THE LADY, OR THE TIGER?

AND OTHER STORIES

BY

FRANK R. STOCKTON

NEW YORK

CHARLES SCRIBNER'S SONS

1887

Franklin Press:
RAND, AVERY, AND COMPANY,
BOSTON.

CONTENTS.

▼

THE LADY, OR THE TIGER?

IN the very olden time, there lived a semi-barbaric king, whose ideas, though somewhat polished and sharpened by the progressiveness of distant Latin neighbors, were still large, florid, and untrammelled, as became the half of him which was barbaric. He was a man of exuberant fancy, and, withal, of an authority so irresistible that, at his will, he turned his varied fancies into facts. He was greatly given to self-communing; and, when he and himself agreed upon any thing, the thing was done. When every member of his domestic and political systems moved smoothly in its appointed course, his nature was bland and genial; but whenever there was a little hitch, and some of his orbs got out of their orbits, he was blander and more genial still, for nothing pleased him so much as to make the crooked straight, and crush down uneven places.

Among the borrowed notions by which his barbarism had become semified was that of the public arena, in which, by exhibitions of manly and beastly valor, the minds of his subjects were refined and cultured.

1

But even here the exuberant and barbaric fancy asserted itself. The arena of the king was built, not to give the people an opportunity of hearing the rhapsodies of dying gladiators, nor to enable them to view the inevitable conclusion of a conflict between religious opinions and hungry jaws, but for purposes far better adapted to widen and develop the mental energies of the people. This vast amphitheatre, with its encircling galleries, its mysterious vaults, and its unseen passages, was an agent of poetic justice, in which crime was punished, or virtue rewarded, by the decrees of an impartial and incorruptible chance.

When a subject was accused of a crime of sufficient importance to interest the king, public notice was given that on an appointed day the fate of the accused person would be decided in the king's arena, — a structure which well deserved its name ; for, although its form and plan were borrowed from afar, its purpose emanated solely from the brain of this man, who, every barleycorn a king, knew no tradition to which he owed more allegiance than pleased his fancy, and who ingrafted on every adopted form of human thought and action the rich growth of his barbaric idealism.

When all the people had assembled in the galleries, and the king, surrounded by his court, sat high up on his throne of royal state on one side of the arena, he gave a signal, a door beneath him opened, and the accused subject stepped out into the amphitheatre. Directly opposite him, on the other side of the enclosed space, were two doors, exactly alike and side by side. It was the duty and the privilege of the person on trial, to walk directly to these doors and open one of them. He could open either door he pleased : he was subject to no guidance or influence but that of the aforementioned impartial and incorruptible chance. If he opened the one, there came out of it a hungry tiger, the fiercest and most cruel that could be procured, which immediately sprang upon him, and tore him to pieces, as a punishment for his guilt. The moment that the case of the criminal was thus decided, doleful iron bells were clanged, great wails went up from the hired mourners posted on the outer rim of the arena, and the vast audience, with bowed heads and downcast hearts, wended slowly their homeward way, mourning greatly that one so young and fair, or so old and respected, should have merited so dire a fate.

But, if the accused person opened the other door, there came forth from it a lady, the most suitable to his years and station that his majesty could select among his fair subjects ; and to this lady he was immediately married, as a reward of his innocence. It mattered not that he might already possess a wife and family, or that his affections might be engaged upon an object of his own selection : the king allowed no such subordinate arrangements to interfere with his great scheme of retribution and reward. The exercises, as in the other instance, took place immediately, and in the arena. Another door opened beneath the king, and a priest, followed by a band of choristers, and dancing maidens blowing joyous airs on golden horns and treading an epithalamic measure, advanced to where the pair stood, side by side ; and the wedding

was promptly and cheerily solemnized. Then the gay
brass bells rang forth their merry peals, the people
shouted glad hurrahs, and the innocent man, preceded
by children strewing flowers on his path, led his bride
to his home.

This was the king's semi-barbaric method of admin-
istering justice. Its perfect fairness is obvious. The
criminal could not know out of which door would come
the lady : he opened either he pleased, without having
the slightest idea whether, in the next instant, he was
to be devoured or married. On some occasions the
tiger came out of one door, and on some out of the
other. The decisions of this tribunal were not only
fair, they were positively determinate : the accused
person was instantly punished if he found himself
guilty ; and, if innocent, he was rewarded on the spot,
whether he liked it or not. There was no escape from
the judgments of the king's arena.

The institution was a very popular one. When the
people gathered together on one of the great trial
days, they never knew whether they were to witness a
bloody slaughter or a hilarious wedding. This element
of uncertainty lent an interest to the occasion which it
could not otherwise have attained. Thus, the masses
were entertained and pleased, and the thinking part of
the community could bring no charge of unfairness
against this plan ; for did not the accused person
have the whole matter in his own hands?

This semi-barbaric king had a daughter as blooming
as his most florid fancies, and with a soul as fervent
and imperious as his own. As is usual in such cases,

she was the apple of his eye, and was loved by him
above all humanity. Among his courtiers was a young
man of that fineness of blood and lowness of station
common to the conventional heroes of romance who
love royal maidens. This royal maiden was well satisfied with her lover, for he was handsome and brave to a
degree unsurpassed in all this kingdom ; and she loved
him with an ardor that had enough of barbarism in it
to make it exceedingly warm and strong. This love
affair moved on happily for many months, until one
day the king happened to discover its existence. He
did not hesitate nor waver in regard to his duty in the
premises. The youth was immediately cast into prison,
and a day was appointed for his trial in the king's
arena. This, of course, was an especially important
occasion ; and his majesty, as well as all the people,
was greatly interested in the workings and development of this trial. Never before had such a case
occurred ; never before had a subject dared to love
the daughter of a king. In after-years such things
became commonplace enough ; but then they were, in
no slight degree, novel and startling.

The tiger-cages of the kingdom were searched for
the most savage and relentless beasts, from which the
fiercest monster might be selected for the arena ; and
the ranks of maiden youth and beauty throughout the
land were carefully surveyed by competent judges, in
order that the young man might have a fitting bride in
case fate did not determine for him a different destiny.
Of course, everybody knew that the deed with which
the accused was charged had been done. He had

loved the princess, and ueither he, she, nor any one else thought of denying the fact; but the king would not think of allowing any fact of this kind to interfere with the workings of the tribunal, in which he took such great delight and satisfaction. No matter how the affair turned out, the youth would be disposed of; and the king would take an æsthetic pleasure in watching the course of events, which would determine whether or not the young man had done wrong in allowing himself to love the princess.

The appointed day arrived. From far and near the people gathered, and thronged the great galleries of the arena; and crowds, unable to gain admittance, massed themselves against its outside walls. The king and his court were in their places, opposite the twin doors, — those fateful portals, so terrible in their similarity.

All was ready. The signal was given. A door beneath the royal party opened, and the lover of the princess walked into the arena. Tall, beautiful, fair, his appearance was greeted with a low hum of admiration and anxiety. Half the audience had not known so grand a youth had lived among them. No wonder the princess loved him! What a terrible thing for him to be there!

As the youth advanced into the arena, he turned, as the custom was, to bow to the king: but he did not think at all of that royal personage; his eyes were fixed upon the princess, who sat to the right of her father. Had it not been for the moiety of barbarism in her nature, it is probable that lady would not have

been there ; but her intense and fervid soul would not
allow her to be absent on an occasion in which she
was so terribly interested.   From the moment that the
decree had gone forth, that her lover should decide his
fate in the king's arena, she had thought of nothing,
night or day, but this great event and the various subjects connected with it.   Possessed of more power,
influence, and force of character than any one who
had ever before been interested in such a case, she had
done what no other person had done, — she had possessed herself of the secret of the doors.   She knew in
which of the two rooms, that lay behind those doors,
stood the cage of the tiger, with its open front, and in
which waited the lady.   Through these thick doors,
heavily curtained with skins on the inside, it was
impossible that any noise or suggestion should come
from within to the person who should approach to
raise the latch of one of them ; but gold, and the
power of a woman's will, had brought the secret to
the princess.

And not only did she know in which room stood the
lady ready to emerge, all blushing and radiant, should
her door be opened, but she knew who the lady was.
It was one of the fairest and loveliest of the damsels
of the court who had been selected as the reward of
the accused youth, should he be proved innocent of the
crime of aspiring to one so far above him ; and the
princess hated her.   Often had she seen, or imagined
that she had seen, this fair creature throwing glances
of admiration upon the person of her lover, and sometimes she thought these glances were perceived and

even returned.   Now and then she had seen them talking together; it was but for a moment or two, but
much can be said in a brief space; it may have been
on most unimportant topics, but how could she know
that?   The girl was lovely, but she had dared to raise
her eyes to the loved one of the princess; and, with
all the intensity of the savage blood transmitted to her
through long lines of wholly barbaric ancestors, she
hated the woman who blushed and trembled behind
that silent door.

When her lover turned and looked at her, and his eye
met hers as she sat there paler and whiter than any one
in the vast ocean of anxious faces about her, he saw,
by that power of quick perception which is given to
those whose souls are one, that she knew behind which
door crouched the tiger, and behind which stood the
lady.   He had expected her to know it.   He understood her nature, and his soul was assured that she
would never rest until she had made plain to herself
this thing, hidden to all other lookers-on, even to the
king.   The only hope for the youth in which there was
any element of certainty was based upon the success
of the princess in discovering this mystery; and the
moment he looked upon her, he saw she had succeeded,
as in his soul he knew she would succeed.

Then it was that his quick and anxious glance asked
the question: "Which?"   It was as plain to her as
if he shouted it from where he stood.   There was not
an instant to be lost.   The question was asked in a
flash; it must be answered in another.

Her right arm lay on the cushioned parapet before

her. She raised her hand, and made a slight, quick movement toward the right. No one but her lover saw her. Every eye but his was fixed on the man in the arena.

He turned, and with a firm and rapid step he walked across the empty space. Every heart stopped beating, every breath was held, every eye was fixed immovably upon that man. Without the slightest hesitation, he went to the door on the right, and opened it.

Now, the point of the story is this: Did the tiger come out of that door, or did the lady?

The more we reflect upon this question, the harder it is to answer. It involves a study of the human heart which leads us through devious mazes of passion, out of which it is difficult to find our way. Think of it, fair reader, not as if the decision of the question depended upon yourself, but upon that hot-blooded, semi-barbaric princess, her soul at a white heat beneath the combined fires of despair and jealousy. She had lost him, but who should have him?

How often, in her waking hours and in her dreams, had she started in wild horror, and covered her face with her hands as she thought of her lover opening the door on the other side of which waited the cruel fangs of the tiger!

But how much oftener had she seen him at the other door! How in her grievous reveries had she gnashed her teeth, and torn her hair, when she saw his start of rapturous delight as he opened the door of the lady! How her soul had burned in agony when she had seen

him rush to meet that woman, with her flushing cheek
and sparkling eye of triumph; when she had seen him
lead her forth, his whole frame kindled with the joy of
recovered life; when she had heard the glad shouts
from the multitude, and the wild ringing of the happy
bells; when she had seen the priest, with his joyous
followers, advance to the couple, and make them man
and wife before her very eyes; and when she had seen
them walk away together upon their path of flowers, followed by the tremendous shouts of the hilarious multitude, in which her one despairing shriek was lost and
drowned!

Would it not be better for him to die at once, and
go to wait for her in the blessed regions of semi-
barbaric futurity?

And yet, that awful tiger, those shrieks, that blood!

Her decision had been indicated in an instant, but
it had been made after days and nights of anguished
deliberation. She had known she would be asked, she
had decided what she would answer, and, without the
slightest hesitation, she had moved her hand to the
right.

The question of her decision is one not to be lightly
considered, and it is not for me to presume to set myself up as the one person able to answer it. And so I
leave it with all of you: Which came out of the opened
door, — the lady, or the tiger?

THE TRANSFERRED GHOST.

THE country residence of Mr. John Hinckman was a delightful place to me, for many reasons. It was the abode of a genial, though somewhat impulsive, hospitality. It had broad, smooth-shaven lawns and towering oaks and elms; there were bosky shades at several points, and not far from the house there was a little rill spanned by a rustic bridge with the bark on; there were fruits and flowers, pleasant people, chess, billiards, rides, walks, and fishing. These were great attractions; but none of them, nor all of them together, would have been sufficient to hold me to the place very long. I had been invited for the trout season, but should, probably, have finished my visit early in the summer had it not been that upon fair days, when the grass was dry, and the sun was not too hot, and there was but little wind, there strolled beneath the lofty elms, or passed lightly through the bosky shades, the form of my Madeline.

This lady was not, in very truth, my Madeline. She had never given herself to me, nor had I, in any way, acquired possession of her. But as I considered her

11

possession the only sufficient reason for the continuance of my existence, I called her, in my reveries, mine. It may have been that I would not have been obliged to confine the use of this possessive pronoun to my reveries had I confessed the state of my feelings to the lady.

But this was an unusually difficult thing to do. Not only did I dread, as almost all lovers dread, taking the step which would in an instant put an end to that delightful season which may be termed the ante-interrogatory period of love, and which might at the same time terminate all intercourse or connection with the object of my passion ; but I was, also, dreadfully afraid of John Hinckman. This gentleman was a good friend of mine, but it would have required a bolder man than I was at that time to ask him for the gift of his niece, who was the head of his household, and, according to his own frequent statement, the main prop of his declining years. Had Madeline acquiesced in my general views on the subject, I might have felt encouraged to open the matter to Mr. Hinckman ; but, as I said before, I had never asked her whether or not she would be mine. I thought of these things at all hours of the day and night, particularly the latter.

I was lying awake one night, in the great bed in my spacious chamber, when, by the dim light of the new moon, which partially filled the room, I saw John Hinckman standing by a large chair near the door. I was very much surprised at this for two reasons. In the first place, my host had never before come into my room ; and, in the second place, he had gone from home that morning, and had not expected to return for several days. It was for this reason that I had been able that evening to sit much later than usual with Madeline on the moonlit porch. The figure was certainly that of John Hinckman in his ordinary dress, but there was a vagueness and indistinctness about it which presently assured me that it was a ghost. Had the good old man been murdered? and had his spirit come to tell me of the deed, and to confide to me the protection of his dear ——? My heart fluttered at what I was about to think, but at this instant the figure spoke.

"Do you know," he said, with a countenance that indicated anxiety, "if Mr. Hinckman will return to-night?"

I thought it well to maintain a calm exterior, and I answered,—

"We do not expect him."

"I am glad of that," said he, sinking into the chair by which he stood. "During the two years and a half that I have inhabited this house, that man has never before been away for a single night. You can't imagine the relief it gives me."

And as he spoke he stretched out his legs, and leaned back in the chair. His form became less vague, and the colors of his garments more distinct and evident, while an expression of gratified relief succeeded to the anxiety of his countenance.

"Two years and a half!" I exclaimed. "I don't understand you."

"It is fully that length of time," said the ghost, "since I first came here. Mine is not an ordinary case. But before I say any thing more about it, let me ask you again if you are sure Mr. Hinckman will not return to-night."

"I am as sure of it as I can be of any thing," I answered. "He left to-day for Bristol, two hundred miles away."

"Then I will go on," said the ghost, "for I am glad to have the opportunity of talking to some one who will listen to me; but if John Hinckman should come in and catch me here, I should be frightened out of my wits."

"This is all very strange," I said, greatly puzzled by what I had heard. "Are you the ghost of Mr. Hinckman?"

This was a bold question, but my mind was so full of other emotions that there seemed to be no room for that of fear.

"Yes, I am his ghost," my companion replied, "and yet I have no right to be. And this is what makes me so uneasy, and so much afraid of him. It is a strange story, and, I truly believe, without precedent. Two years and a half ago, John Hinckman was dangerously ill in this very room. At one time he was so far gone that he was really believed to be dead. It was in consequence of too precipitate a report in regard to this matter that I was, at that time, appointed to be his ghost. Imagine my surprise and horror, sir, when, after I had accepted the position and assumed its responsibilities, that old man revived, became convalescent, and eventually regained his usual health. My situation was now one of extreme delicacy and embarrassment. I had no power to return to my original unembodiment, and I had no right to be the ghost of a man who was not dead. I was advised by my friends to quietly maintain my position, and was assured that, as John Hinckman was an elderly man, it could not be long before I could rightfully assume the position for which I had been selected. But I tell you, sir," he continued, with animation, "the old fellow seems as vigorous as ever, and I have no idea how much longer this annoying state of things will continue. I spend my time trying to get out of that old man's way. I must not leave this house, and he seems to follow me everywhere. I tell you, sir, he haunts me."

"That is truly a queer state of things," I remarked. "But why are you afraid of him? He couldn't hurt you."

"Of course he couldn't," said the ghost. "But his very presence is a shock and terror to me. Imagine, sir, how you would feel if my case were yours."

I could not imagine such a thing at all. I simply shuddered.

"And if one must be a wrongful ghost at all," the apparition continued, "it would be much pleasanter to be the ghost of some man other than John Hinckman. There is in him an irascibility of temper, accompanied by a facility of invective, which is seldom met with. And what would happen if he were to see me, and find out, as I am sure he would, how long and why I had inhabited his house, I can scarcely conceive. I have seen him in his bursts of passion; and, although he did not hurt the people he stormed at any more than he would hurt me, they seemed to shrink before him.''

All this I knew to be very true. Had it not been for this peculiarity of Mr. Hinckman, I might have been more willing to talk to him about his niece.

"I feel sorry for you," I said, for I really began to have a sympathetic feeling toward this unfortunate apparition. "Your case is indeed a hard one. It reminds me of those persons who have had doubles, and I suppose a man would often be very angry indeed when he found that there was another being who was personating himself."

''Oh! the cases are not similar at all," said the ghost. "A double or doppelganger lives on the earth with a man ; and, being exactly like him, he makes all sorts of trouble, of course. It is very different with me. I am not here to live with Mr. Hinckman. I am here to take his place. Now, it would make John Hinckman very angry if he knew that. Don't you know it would?"

I assented promptly.

"Now that he is away I can be easy for a little while," continued the ghost; "and I am so glad to have an opportunity of talking to you. I have frequently come into your room, and watched you while you slept, but did not dare to speak to you for fear that if you talked with me Mr. Hinckman would hear you, and come into the room to know why you were talking to yourself."

''But would he not hear you?'' I asked.

''Oh, no!'' said the other: '' there are times when

any one may see me, but no one hears me except the person to whom I address myself.''

'' But why did you wish to speak to me?'' I asked.

'' Because,'' replied the ghost, '' I like occasionally to talk to people, and especially to some one like yourself, whose mind is so troubled and perturbed that you are not likely to be frightened by a visit from one of us. But I particularly wanted to ask you to do me a favor. There is every probability, so far as I can see, that John Hinckman will live a long time, and my situation is becoming insupportable. My great object at present is to get myself transferred, and I think that you may, perhaps, be of use to me.''

'' Transferred!'' I exclaimed. '' What do you mean by that?''

'' What I mean,'' said the other, '' is this: Now that I have started on my career I have got to be the ghost of somebody, and I want to be the ghost of a man who is really dead.''

'' I should think that would be easy enough.'' I said. '' Opportunities must continually occur.''

'' Not at all! not at all!'' said my companion quickly. '' You have no idea what a rush and pressure there is for situations of this kind. Whenever a vacancy occurs, if I may express myself in that way, there are crowds of applications for the ghostship.''

'' I had no idea that such a state of things existed,'' I said, becoming quite interested in the matter. '' There ought to be some regular system, or order of precedence, by which you could all take your turns like customers in a barber's shop.''

"Oh dear, that would never do at all!" said the other. "Some of us would have to wait forever. There is always a great rush whenever a good ghost-ship offers itself — while, as you know, there are some positions that no one would care for. And it was in consequence of my being in too great a hurry on an occasion of the kind that I got myself into my present disagreeable predicament, and I have thought that it might be possible that you would help me out of it. You might know of a case where an opportunity for a ghostship was not generally expected, but which might present itself at any moment. If you would give me a short notice, I know I could arrange for a transfer."

"What do you mean?" I exclaimed. "Do you want me to commit suicide? Or to undertake a murder for your benefit?"

"Oh, no, no, no!" said the other, with a vapory smile. "I mean nothing of that kind. To be sure, there are lovers who are watched with considerable interest, such persons having been known, in moments of depression, to offer very desirable ghostships ; but I did not think of any thing of that kind in connection with you. You were the only person I cared to speak to, and I hoped that you might give me some information that would be of use ; and, in return, I shall be very glad to help you in your love affair."

"You seem to know that I have such an affair," I said.

"Oh, yes!" replied the other, with a little yawn. "I could not be here so much as I have been without knowing all about that."

There was something horrible in the idea of Madeline and myself having been watched by a ghost, even,
perhaps, when we wandered together in the most delightful and bosky places. But, then, this was quite
an exceptional ghost, and I could not have the objections to him which would ordinarily arise in regard to
beings of his class.

"I must go now," said the ghost, rising: "but I
will see you somewhere to-morrow night. And remember — you help me, and I'll help you."

I had doubts the next morning as to the propriety
of telling Madeline any thing about this interview, and
soon convinced myself that I must keep silent on the
subject. If she knew there was a ghost about the
house, she would probably leave the place instantly. I
did not mention the matter, and so regulated my demeanor that I am quite sure Madeline never suspected
what had taken place. For some time I had wished
that Mr. Hinckman would absent himself, for a day
at least, from the premises. In such case I thought
I might more easily nerve myself up to the point of
speaking to Madeline on the subject of our future col-
lateral existence; and, now that the opportunity for
such speech had really occurred, I did not feel ready
to avail myself of it. What would become of me if
she refused me?

I had an idea, however, that the lady thought that,
if I were going to speak at all, this was the time. She
must have known that certain sentiments were afloat
within me, and she was not unreasonable in her wish
to see the matter settled one way or the other. But I

did not feel like taking a bold step in the dark. If
she wished me to ask her to give herself to me, she
ought to offer me some reason to suppose that she
would make the gift. If I saw no probability of such
generosity, I would prefer that things should remain as
they were.

That evening I was sitting with Madeline in the
moonlit porch. It was nearly ten o'clock, and ever
since supper-time I had been working myself up to
the point of making an avowal of my sentiments. I
had not positively determined to do this, but wished
gradually to reach the proper point, when, if the prospect looked bright, I might speak. My companion
appeared to understand the situation — at least, I imagined that the nearer I came to a proposal the more
she seemed to expect it. It was certainly a very criti-
cal and important epoch in my life. If I spoke, I
should make myself happy or miserable forever; and
if I did not speak I had every reason to believe that
the lady would not give me another chance to do so.
Sitting thus with Madeline, talking a little, and
thinking very hard over these momentous matters, I
looked up and saw the ghost. not a dozen feet away
from us. He was sitting on the railing of the porch,
one leg thrown up before him, the other dangling down
as he leaned against a post. He was behind Madeline,
but almost in front of me, as I sat facing the lady.
It was fortunate that Madeline was looking out over
the landscape, for I must have appeared very much
startled. The ghost had told me that he would see me

some time this night, but I did not think he would
make his appearance when I was in the company of
Madeline. If she should see the spirit of her uncle, I
could not answer for the consequences. I made no
exclamation, but the ghost evidently saw that I was
troubled.

"Don't be afraid," he said — "I shall not let her
see me; and she cannot hear me speak unless I address myself to her, which I do not intend to do."

I suppose I looked grateful.

"So you need not trouble yourself about that," the
ghost continued; "but it seems to me that you are not
getting along very well with your affair. If I were
you, I should speak out without waiting any longer.
You will never have a better chance. You are not
likely to be interrupted; and, so far as I can judge,
the lady seems disposed to listen to you favorably;
that is, if she ever intends to do so. There is no
knowing when John Hinckman will go away again;
certainly not this summer. If I were in your place, I
should never dare to make love to Hinckman's niece if
he were anywhere about the place. If he should catch
any one offering himself to Miss Madeline, he would
then be a terrible man to encounter."

I agreed perfectly to all this.

"I cannot bear to think of him!" I ejaculated
aloud.

"Think of whom?" asked Madeline, turning quickly toward me.

Here was an awkward situation. The long speech
of the ghost, to which Madeline paid no attention, but

which I heard with perfect distinctness, had made me forget myself.

It was necessary to explain quickly. Of course, it would not do to admit that it was of her dear uncle that I was speaking; and so I mentioned hastily the first name I thought of.

" Mr. Vilars," I said.

This statement was entirely correct; for I never could bear to think of Mr. Vilars, who was a gentleman who had, at various times, paid much attention to Madeline.

" It is wrong for you to speak in that way of Mr. Vilars," she said. " He is a remarkably well educated and sensible young man, and has very pleasant manners. He expects to be elected to the legislature this fall, and I should not be surprised if he made his mark. He will do well in a legislative body, for whenever Mr. Vilars has any thing to say he knows just how and when to say it."

This was spoken very quietly, and without any show of resentment, which was all very natural, for if Madeline thought at all favorably of me she could not feel displeased that I should have disagreeable emotions in regard to a possible rival. The concluding words contained a hint which I was not slow to understand. I felt very sure that if Mr. Vilars were in my present position he would speak quickly enough.

" I know it is wrong to have such ideas about a person," I said, " but I cannot help it."

The lady did not chide me, and after this she seemed even in a softer mood. As for me, I felt considerably annoyed, for I had not wished to admit that any thought of Mr. Vilars had ever occupied my mind.

"You should not speak aloud that way," said the ghost, "or you may get yourself into trouble. I want to see every thing go well with you, because then you may be disposed to help me, especially if I should chance to be of any assistance to you, which I hope I shall be."

I longed to tell him that there was no way in which he could help me so much as by taking his instant departure. To make love to a young lady with a ghost sitting on the railing near by, and that ghost the apparition of a much-dreaded uncle, the very idea of whom in such a position and at such a time made me tremble, was a difficult, if not an impossible, thing to do ; but I forbore to speak, although I may have looked my mind.

"1 suppose," continued the ghost, "that you have not heard any thing that might be of advantage to me. Of course, I am very anxious to hear ; but if you have any thing to tell me, I can wait until you are alone. I will come to you to-night in your room, or I will stay here until the lady goes away."

"You need not wait here," I said ; "I have nothing at all to say to you."

Madeline sprang to her feet, her face flushed and her eyes ablaze.

"Wait here !" she cried. "What do you suppose I am waiting for? Nothing to say to me indeed ! — I should think so ! What should you have to say to me? "

"Madeline," I exclaimed, stepping toward her, "let me explain."

But she had gone.

Here was the end of the world for me! I turned fiercely to the ghost.

"Wretched existence!" I cried. "You - have ruined every thing. You have blackened my whole life. Had it not been for you " ——

But here my voice faltered. I could say no more.

"You wrong me," said the ghost. "I have not injured you. I have tried only to encourage and assist you, and it is your own folly that has done this mischief. But do not despair. Such mistakes as these can be explained. Keep up a brave heart. Good-by."

And he vanished from the railing like a bursting soap-bubble.

I went gloomily to bed, but I saw no apparitions that night except those of despair and misery which my wretched thoughts called up. The words I had uttered had sounded to Madeline like the basest insult. Of course, there was only one interpretation she could put upon them.

As to explaining my ejaculations, that was impossible. I thought the matter over and over again as I lay awake that night, and I determined that I would never tell Madeline the facts of the case. It would be better for me to suffer all my life than for her to know that the ghost of her uncle haunted the house. Mr. Hinckman was away, and if she knew of his ghost she could not be made to believe that he was not dead.

She might not survive the shock! No, my heart could bleed, but I would never tell her.

The next day was fine, neither too cool nor too warm; the breezes were gentle, and nature smiled. But there were no walks or rides with Madeline. She seemed to be much engaged during the day, and I saw but little of her. When we met at meals she was polite, but very quiet and reserved. She had evidently determined on a course of conduct, and had resolved to assume that, although I had been very rude to her, she did not understand the import of my words. It would be quite proper, of course, for her not to know what I meant by my expressions of the night before.

I was downcast and wretched, and said but little, and the only bright streak across the black horizon of my woe was the fact that she did not appear to be happy, although she affected an air of unconcern. The moonlit porch was deserted that evening, but wandering about the house I found Madeline in the library alone. She was reading, but I went in and sat down near her. I felt that, although I could not do so fully, I must in a measure explain my conduct of the night before. She listened quietly to a somewhat labored apology I made for the words I had used.

"I have not the slightest idea what you meant," she said, "but you were very rude."

I earnestly disclaimed any intention of rudeness, and assured her, with a warmth of speech that must have made some impression upon her, that rudeness to her would be an action impossible to me. I said a great deal upon the subject, and implored her to believe that if it were not for a certain obstacle I could speak to her so plainly that she would understand every thing.

She was silent for a time, and then she said, rather more kindly, I thought, than she had spoken before :

"Is that obstacle in any way connected with my uncle?"

"Yes," I answered, after a little hesitation, "it is, in a measure, connected with him."

She made no answer to this, and sat looking at her book, but not reading. From the expression of her face, I thought she was somewhat softened toward me. She knew her uncle as well as I did, and she may have been thinking that, if he were the obstacle that prevented my speaking (and there were many ways in which he might be that obstacle), my position would be such a hard one that it would excuse some wildness of speech and eccentricity of manner. I saw, too, that the warmth of my partial explanations had had some effect on her, and I began to believe that it might be a good thing for me to speak my mind without delay. No matter how she should receive my proposition, my relations with her could not be worse than they had been the previous night and day, and there was something in her face which encouraged me to hope that she might forget my foolish exclamations of the evening before if I began to tell her my tale of love.

I drew my chair a little nearer to her, and as I did so the ghost burst into the room from the door-way behind her. I say burst, although no door flew open and he made no noise. He was wildly excited, and waved his arms above his head. The moment I saw him, my heart fell within me. With the entrance of that impertinent apparition, every hope fled from me. I could not speak while he was in the room.

I must have turned pale; and I gazed steadfastly at the ghost, almost without seeing Madeline, who sat between us.

"Do you know," he cried, "that John Hinckman is coming up the hill? He will be here in fifteen minutes; and if you are doing any thing in the way of love-making, you had better hurry it up. But this is not what I came to tell you. I have glorious news! At last I am transferred! Not forty minutes ago a Russian nobleman was murdered by the Nihilists. Nobody ever thought of him in connection with an immediate ghostship. My friends instantly applied for the situation for me, and obtained my transfer. I am off before that horrid Hinckman comes up the hill. The moment I reach my new position, I shall put off this hated semblance. Good-by. You can't imagine how glad I am to be, at last, the real ghost of somebody."

"Oh!" I cried, rising to my feet, and stretching out my arms in utter wretchedness, "I would to Heaven you were mine!"

"I *am* yours," said Madeline, raising to me her tearful eyes.

THE SPECTRAL MORTGAGE.

TOWARD the close of a beautiful afternoon in early summer 1 stood on the piazza of the spacious country-house which was my home. I had just dined, and I gazed with a peculiar comfort and delight upon the wide-spreading lawn and the orchards and groves beyond; and then, walking to the other end of the piazza, I looked out toward the broad pastures, from which a fine drove of cattle were leisurely coming home to be milked, and toward the fields of grain, whose green was beginning already to be touched with yellow. Involuntarily (for, on principle, I was opposed to such feelings) a pleasant sense of possession came over me. It could not be long before all this would virtually be mine.

About two years before, I had married the niece of John Hinckman, the owner of this fine estate. He was very old, and could not be expected to survive much longer, and had willed the property, without reserve, to my wife. This, in brief, was the cause of my present sense of prospective possession; and although, as I said, I was principled against the voluntary encouragement of such a sentiment, I could not blame myself if the feeling occasionally arose within me. I had not married my wife for her uncle's money. Indeed, we had both expected that the marriage would result in her being entirely disinherited. His niece was John Hinckman's housekeeper and sole prop and comfort, and if she left him for me she expected no kindness at his hands. But she had not left him. To our surprise, her uncle invited us to live with him, and our relations with him became more and more amicable and pleasant, and Mr. Hinckman had, of late, frequently expressed to me his great satisfaction that I had proved to be a man after his own heart; that I took an interest in flocks and herds and crops; that I showed a talent for such pursuits; and that I would continue to give, when he was gone, the same care and attention to the place which it had been so long his greatest pleasure to bestow. He was old and ill now, and tired of it all; and the fact that I had not proved to be, as he had formerly supposed me, a mere city gentleman, was a great comfort to his declining days. We were deeply grieved to think that the old man must soon die. We would gladly have kept him with us for years; but, if he must go, it was pleasant to know that he and ourselves were so well satisfied with the arrangements that had been made. Think me not cold and heartless, high-minded reader. For a few moments put yourself in my place.

But had you, at that time, put yourself in my place on that pleasant piazza, I do not believe you would have cared to stay there long; for, as I stood gazing over the fields, I felt a touch upon my shoulder. I cannot say that I was actually touched, but I experienced a feeling which indicated that the individual who had apparently touched me would have done so had he been able. I instantly turned, and saw, standing beside me, a tall figure in the uniform of a Russian officer. I started back, but made no sound. I knew what the figure was. It was a spectre — a veritable ghost.

Some years before this place had been haunted. I knew this well, for I had seen the ghost myself. But before my marriage the spectre had disappeared, and had not been seen since ; and I must admit that my satisfaction, when thinking of this estate, without mortgage or incumbrance, was much increased by the thought that even the ghost, who used to haunt the house, had now departed.

But here he was again. Although in different form and guise, I knew him. It was the same ghost.

" Do you remember me? " said the figure.

" Yes," I answered : " I remember you in the form in which you appeared to me some time ago. Although your aspect is entirely changed, I feel you to be the same ghost that I have met before."

" You are right," said the spectre. " I am glad to see you looking so well, and apparently happy. But John Hinckman, I understand, is in a very low state of health."

" Yes," I said : " he is very old and ill. But I hope," I continued, as a cloud of anxiety began to rise within me, " that his expected decease has no connection with any prospects or plans of your own."

" No," said the ghost. " I am perfectly satisfied
with my present position. I am off duty during the
day ; and the difference in time between this country
and Russia gives me opportunities of being here in
your early evening, and of visiting scenes and localities
which are very familiar and agreeable to me."

" Which fact, perhaps, you had counted upon when
you first put this uniform on," I remarked.

The ghost smiled.

" I must admit, however," he said, " that I am
seeking this position for a friend of mine, and I have
reason to believe that he will obtain it."

" Good heavens!" I exclaimed. " Is it possible
that this house is to be haunted by a ghost as soon as
the old gentleman expires? Why should this family
be tormented in such a horrible way? Everybody who
dies does not have a ghost walking about his house."

" Oh, no!" said the spectre. " There are thousands
of positions of the kind which are never applied for ;
but the ghostship here is a very desirable one, and
there are many applicants for it. I think you will like
my friend, if he gets it."

" Like him!" I groaned.

The idea was horrible to me.

The ghost evidently perceived how deeply I was
affected by what he had said, for there was a compas-
sionate expression on his countenance. As I looked
at him an idea struck me. If I were to have any
ghost at all about the house, I would prefer this one.
Could there be such things as duplex ghostships?
Since it was day here when it was night in Russia,

why could not this spectre serve in both places? It was common enough for a person to fill two situations. The notion seemed feasible to me, and I broached it.

"Thank you," said the ghost. "But the matter cannot be arranged in that way. Night and day are not suitably divided between here and Russia; and, besides, it is necessary for the incumbent of this place to be on duty at all hours. You remember that I came to you by day as well as at night?"

Oh, yes! I remembered that. It was additionally unfortunate that the ghostship here should not be one of the limited kind.

"Why is it," I asked, "that a man's own spirit does not attend to these matters? I always thought that was the way the thing was managed."

The ghost shook his head.

"Consider for a moment," here plied, "what chance a man's own spirit, without experience and without influence, would have in a crowd of importunate applicants, versed in all the arts, and backed by the influence necessary in such a contest. Of course there are cases in which a person becomes his own ghost; but this is because the position is undesirable, and there is no competition."

"And this new-comer," I exclaimed, in much trouble, "will he take the form of Mr. Hinckman? If my wife should see such an apparition it would kill her."

"The ghost who will haunt this place," said my companion, "will not appear in the form of John Hinckman. I am glad that is so, if it will please you;

for you are the only man with whom I have ever held such unrestrained and pleasant intercourse. Good-by."

And with these words no figure of a Russian officer stood before me.

For some minutes I remained motionless, with downcast eyes, a very different man from the one who had just gazed out with such delight over the beautiful landscape. A shadow, not that of night, had fallen over every thing. This fine estate was not to come to us clear and unencumbered, as we thought. It was to be saddled with a horrible lien, a spectral mortgage.

Madeline had gone up stairs with Pegram. Pegram was our baby. I disliked his appellation with all my heart; but Pegram was a family name on Madeline's side of the house, and she insisted that our babe should bear it. Madeline was very much wrapped up in Pegram, often I thought too much so; for there were many times when I should have been very glad of my wife's society, but was obliged to do without it because she was entirely occupied with Pegram. To be sure, my wife's sister was with us, and there was a child's nurse; but, for all that, Madeline was so completely Pegramized, that a great many of the hours which I, in my anticipations of matrimonial felicity, had imagined would be passed in the company of my wife, were spent alone, or with the old gentleman, or Belle.

Belle was a fine girl; to me not so charming and attractive as her sister, but perhaps equally so to some other persons, certainly to one. This was Will Crenshaw, an old school-fellow of mine, then a civil engi-

neer, in South America. Will was the declared suitor
of Belle, although she had never formally accepted
him; but Madeline and myself both strongly favored
the match, and felt very anxious that she should do
so, and indeed were quite certain that when Will
should return every thing would be made all right.
The young engineer was a capital fellow, had excellent
prospects, and was my best friend. It was our plan
that after their marriage the youthful couple should
live with us. This, of course, would be delightful to
both Belle and her sister, and I could desire no better
companion than Will. He was not to go to distant
countries any more, and who could imagine a pleasanter home than ours would be.

And now here was this dreadful prospect of a
household ghost!

A week or so passed by, and John Hinckman was
no more. Every thing was done for him that respect
and affection could dictate, and no one mourned his
death more heartily than I. If I could have had my
way he would have lived as long as I, myself, remained
upon this earth.

When every thing about the house had settled down
into its accustomed quiet, I began to look out for the
coming of the expected ghost. I felt sure that I
would be the one to whom he would make his appearance, and with my regret and annoyance at his expected coming was mingled a feeling of curiosity to
know in what form he would appear. He was not to
come as John Hinckman — that was the only bit of
comfort in the whole affair.

But several weeks passed, and I saw no ghost; and I began to think that perhaps the aversion I had shown to having such an inmate of my household had had its effect, and I was to be spared the infliction. And now another subject occupied my thoughts. It was summer, the afternoons were pleasant, and on one of them I asked Belle to take a walk with me. I would have preferred Madeline, but she had excused herself as she was very busy making what I presumed to be an altar cloth for Pegram. It turned out to be an afghan for his baby carriage, but the effect was the same: she could not go. When I could not have Madeline I liked very well to walk with Belle. She was a pleasant girl, and in these walks I always talked to her of Crenshaw. My desire that she should marry my friend grew stronger daily. But this afternoon Belle hesitated, and looked a little confused.

"I am not sure that I shall walk to-day."

"But you have your hat on," I urged : "I supposed you had made ready for a walk."

"No," said she : "I thought I would go somewhere with my book."

"You haven't a book," I said, looking at her hands, one of which held a parasol.

"You are dreadfully exact," she replied, with a little laugh : "I am going into the library to get one." And away she ran.

There was something about this I did not like. I firmly believed she had come down stairs prepared to take a walk. But she did not want me ; that was evident enough. I went off for a long walk, and when

I returned supper was ready, but Belle had not appeared.

"She has gone off somewhere with a book," I said. "I'll go and look for her."

I walked down to the bosky grove at the foot of the lawn, and passed through it without seeing any signs of Belle. Soon, however, I caught sight of her light dress in an open space a little distance beyond me. Stepping forward a few paces I had a full view of her, and my astonishment can be imagined when I saw that she was standing in the shade of a tree talking to a young man. His back was turned toward me. but I could see from his figure and general air that he was young. His hat was a little on one side, in his hand he carried a short whip, and he wore a pair of riding-boots. He and Belle were engaged in very earnest conversation, and did not perceive me. I was not only surprised but shocked at the sight. I was quite certain Belle had come here to meet this young man, who, to me, was a total stranger. I did not wish Belle to know that I had seen her with him ; and so I stepped back out of their sight, and began to call her. It was not long before I saw her coming toward me, and, as I expected, alone.

"Indeed," she cried, looking at her watch, "I did not know it was so late."

"Have you had a pleasant time with your book?" I asked, as we walked homeward.

"I wasn't reading all the time," she answered.

I asked her no more questions. It was not for me to begin an inquisition into this matter. But that night I told Madeline all about it. The news troubled her much, and like myself she was greatly grieved at Belle's evident desire to deceive us. When there was a necessity for it my wife could completely de-Pegramize herself, and enter with quick and judicious action into the affairs of others.

"I will go with her to-morrow," she said. "If this person comes, I do not intend that she shall meet him alone."

The next afternoon Belle started out again with her book; but she had gone but a few steps when she was joined by Madeline, with hat and parasol, and together they walked into the bosky grove. They returned in very good time for supper; and as we went in to that meal, Madeline whispered to me:

"There was nobody there."

"And did she say nothing to you of the young man with whom she was talking yesterday?" I asked, when we were alone some hours later.

"Not a word," she said, "though I gave her every opportunity. I wonder if you could have been mistaken."

"I am sure I was not." I replied. "I saw the man as plainly as I see you."

"Then Belle is treating us very badly," she said. "If she desires the company of young men let her say so, and we will invite them to the house."

I did not altogether agree with this latter remark. I did not care to have Belle know young men. I wanted her to marry Will Crenshaw, and be done with it. But we both agreed not to speak to the young lady on the subject. It was not for us to pry into her secrets, and if any thing was to be said she should say it.

Every afternoon Belle went away, as before, with her book ; but we did not accompany her, nor allude to her newly acquired love for solitary walks and studies. One afternoon we had callers, and she could not go. That night, after I had gone to sleep, Madeline awoke me with a little shake.

" Listen," she whispered. " Whom is Belle talking to ? "

The night was warm, and all our doors and windows were open. Belle's chamber was not far from ours ; and we could distinctly hear her speaking in a low tone. She was evidently holding a conversation with some one whose voice we could not hear.

" I'll go in," said Madeline, rising, " and see about this."

" No, no," I whispered. " She is talking to some one outside. Let me go down and speak to him."

I slipped on some clothes and stole quietly down the stairs. I unfastened the back door and went round to the side on which Belle's window opened. No sooner had I reached the corner than I saw, directly under the window, and looking upward, his hat cocked a good deal on one side, and his riding-whip in his hand, the jaunty young fellow with whom I had seen Belle talking.

" Hello ! " I cried, and rushed toward him. At the sound of my voice he turned to me, and I saw his face distinctly. He was young and handsome. There was a sort of half laugh on his countenance, as if he had

just been saying something very witty. But he did
not wait to finish his remark or to speak to me. There
was a large evergreen near him; and, stepping quickly
behind it, he was lost to my view. I ran around the
bush, but could see nothing of him. There was a good
deal of shrubbery hereabouts, and he was easily able
to get away unobserved. I continued the search for
about ten minutes, and then, quite sure that the fellow
had got away, I returned to the house. Madeline had
lighted a lamp, and was calling down-stairs to ask if
I had found the man; some of the servants were up,
and anxious to know what had happened; Pegram was
crying; but in Belle's room all was quiet. Madeline
looked in at the open door, and saw her lying quietly
in her bed. No word was spoken; and my wife
returned to our room, where we discussed the affair
for a long time.

In the morning I determined to give Belle a chance
to speak, and at the breakfast-table I said to her:

"I suppose you heard the disturbance last night?"

"Yes," she said quietly. "Did you catch the
man?"

"No," I answered, with considerable irritation,
"but I wish I had."

"What would you have done if you had caught
him?" she asked, as with unusual slowness and deliberation she poured some cream upon her oat-meal.

"Done!" I exclaimed, "I don't know what I would
have done. But one thing is certain, I would have
made him understand that I would have no strangers
prowling around my house at night."

Belle colored a little at the last part of this remark; but she made no answer, and the subject was dropped.

This conversation greatly pained both Madeline and myself. It made it quite clear to us that Belle was aware that we knew of her acquaintance with this young man, and that she still determined to say nothing to us, either in the way of confidence or excuse. She had treated us badly, and we could not help showing it. On her side Belle was very quiet, and entirely different from the gay girl she had been some time before.

I urged Madeline to go to Belle and speak to her as a sister, but she declined. "No," she said: "I know Belle's spirit, and there would be trouble. If there is to be a quarrel I shall not begin it."

I was determined to end this unpleasant feeling, which, to me, was almost as bad as a quarrel. If the thing were possible I would put an end to the young man's visits. I could never have the same opinion of Belle I had had before; but if this impudent fellow could be kept away, and Will Crenshaw should come back and attend to his business as an earnest suitor ought, all might yet be well.

And now, strange to say, I began to long for the ghost, whose coming had been promised. I had been considering what means I should take to keep Belle's clandestine visitor away, and had found the question rather a difficult one to settle. I could not shoot the man, and it would indeed be difficult to prevent the meeting of two young persons over whom I had no actual control. But I happened to think that if I could get the aid of the expected ghost the matter would be easy. If it should be as accommodating and obliging as the one who had haunted the house before, it would readily agree to forward the fortunes of the family by assisting in breaking up this unfortunate connection. If it would consent to be present at their interviews the affair was settled. I knew from personal experience that love-making in the presence of a ghost was extremely unpleasant, and in this case I believed it would be impossible.

Every night, after the rest of the household had gone to bed, I wandered about the grounds, examining the porches and the balconies, looking up to the chimneys and the ornaments on top of the house, hoping to see that phantom, whose coming I had, a short time before, anticipated with such dissatisfaction and repugnance. If I could even again meet the one who was now serving in Russia, I thought it would answer my purpose as well.

On the third or fourth night after I had begun my nocturnal rounds, I encountered, on a path not very far from the house, the young fellow who had given us so much trouble. My indignation at his impudent reappearance knew no bounds. The moon was somewhat obscured by fleecy clouds; but I could see that he wore the same jaunty air, his hat was cocked a little more on one side, he stood with his feet quite wide apart, and in his hands, clasped behind him, he held his riding-whip. I stepped quickly toward him.

" Well, sir ! " I exclaimed.

He did not seem at all startled.

" How d'ye do ? " he said, with a little nod.

" How dare you, sir," I cried, " intrude yourself on my premises ? This is the second time I have found you here, and now I want you to understand that you are to get away from here just as fast as you can ; and if you are ever caught again anywhere on this estate, I'll have you treated as a trespasser."

" Indeed," said he, " I would be sorry to put you to so much trouble. And now let me say that I have tried to keep out of your way, but since you have proved so determined to make my acquaintance I thought I might come forward and do the sociable."

" None of your impertinence," I cried. " What brings you here, anyway ? "

" Well," said he, with a little laugh, " if you want to know, I don't mind telling you I came to see Miss Belle."

" You confounded rascal ! " I cried, raising my heavy stick. " Get out of my sight, or I will break your head ! "

" All right," said he, " break away ! "

And drawing himself up, he gave his right boot a slap with his whip.

The whip went entirely through both legs ! It was the ghost !

Utterly astounded I started back, and sat down upon a raised flower-bed, against which I had stumbled. I had no strength, nor power to speak. I had seen a ghost before, but I was entirely overcome by this amazing development.

" And now I suppose you know who I am," said the spectre, approaching, and standing in front of me.

"The one who was here before told me that your lady
didn't fancy ghosts, and that I had better keep out of
sight of both of you ; but he didn't say any thing about
Miss Belle : and by George ! sir, it wouldn't have mattered if he had ; for if it hadn't been for that charming
young lady I shouldn't have been here at all. I am
the ghost of Buck Edwards, who was pretty well known
in the lower part of this county about seventy years
ago. I always had a great eye for the ladies, sir, and
when I got a chance to court one I didn't miss it. I
did too much courting, however ; for I roused up a
jealous fellow, named Ruggles, and he shot me in a
duel early one September morning. Since then I have
haunted, from time to time, more than a dozen houses
where there were pretty girls."

"Do you mean to say," I asked, now finding
strength, "that a spirit would care to come back to
this earth to court a girl?"

"Why, what are you thinking of?" exclaimed the
phantom of Buck Edwards. "Do you suppose that
only old misers and lovelorn maidens want to come
back and have a good time? No, sir! Every one of
us, who is worth any thing, comes if he can get a
chance. By George, sir! do you know I courted Miss
Belle's grandmother? And a couple of gay young
ones we were too! Nobody ever knew any thing of
it, and that made it all the livelier."

"Do you intend to stay here and pay attention to
my sister-in-law?" I asked, anxiously.

"Certainly I do," was the reply. "Didn't I say
that is what I came for?"

"Don't you see the mischief you will do?" I asked. "You will probably break off a match between her and a most excellent gentleman whom we all desire" ——

"Break off a match!" exclaimed the ghost of Buck Edwards, with a satisfied grin. "How many matches I have broken off! The last thing I ever did, before I went away, was of that sort. She wouldn't marry the gentleman who shot me." There was evidently no conscience to this spectre.

"And if you do not care for that," I said, in considerable anger, "I can tell you that you are causing ill-feeling between the young lady and the best friends she has in the world, which may end very disastrously."

"Now, look here, my man," said the ghost; "if you and your wife are really her friends you wont act like fools and make trouble."

I made no answer to this remark, but asserted, with much warmth, that I intended to tell Miss Belle exactly what he was, and so break off the engagement at once.

"If you tell her that she's been walking and talking with the ghost of the fellow who courted her grandmother, — I reckon she could find some of my letters now among the old lady's papers if she looked for them, — you'd frighten the wits out of her. She'd go crazy. I know girls' natures, sir."

"So do I," I groaned.

"Don't get excited," he said. "Let the girl alone, and every thing will be comfortable and pleasant. Good-night."

I went to bed, but not to sleep. Here was a terrible situation. A sister-in-law courted by a ghost! Was ever a man called upon to sustain such a trial! And I must sustain it alone. There was no one with whom I could share the secret.

Several times after this I saw this baleful spectre of a young buck of the olden time. He would nod to me with a jocular air, but I did not care to speak to him. One afternoon I went into the house to look for my wife; and, very naturally, I entered the room where Pegram lay in his little bed. The child was asleep, and no one was with him. I stood and gazed contemplatively upon my son. He was a handsome child, and apparently full of noble instincts; and yet I could not help wishing that he were older, or that in some way his conditions were such that it should not be necessary, figuratively speaking, that his mother should continually hover about him. If she could be content with a little less of Pegram and a little more of me, my anticipations of a matrimonial career would be more fully realized.

As these thoughts were passing through my mind I raised my eyes, and on the other side of the little bedstead I saw the wretched ghost of Buck Edwards.

"Fine boy," he said.

My indignation at seeing this impudent existence within the most sacred precincts of my house was boundless.

"You vile interloper!" I cried.

At this moment Madeline entered the room. Pale and stern, she walked directly to the crib and took up the child. Then she turned to me and said:

" I was standing in the door-way, and saw you look-ing at my babe. I heard what you said to him. I have suspected it before." And then, with Pegram in her arms, she strode out of the room.

The ghost had vanished as Madeline entered. Filled with rage and bitterness, for my wife had never spoken to me in these tones before, I ran down-stairs and rushed out of the house. I walked long and far, my mind filled with doleful thoughts. When I returned to the house, I found a note from my wife. It ran thus:

"I have gone to aunt Hannah's with Pegram, and have taken Belle. I cannot live with one who considers my child a vile interloper."

As I sat down in my misery, there was one little spark of comfort amid the gloom. She had taken Belle. My first impulse was to follow into the city and explain every thing; but I quickly reflected that if I did this I must tell her of the ghost, and I felt certain that she would never return with Pegram to a haunted house. Must I, in order to regain my wife, give up this beautiful home? For two days I racked my brains and wandered gloomily about.

In one of my dreary rambles I encountered the ghost. "What are you doing here?" I cried. "Miss Belle has gone."

"I know that," the spectre answered, his air expressing all his usual impertinence and swagger, "but she'll come back. When your wife returns, she's bound to bring young Miss."

At this, a thought flashed through my mind. If any

good would come of it, Belle should never return. Whatever else happened, this insolent ghost of a gay young buck should have no excuse for haunting my house.

"She will never come back while you are here," I cried.

"I don't believe it," it coolly answered.

I made no further assertions on the subject. I had determined what to do, and it was of no use to be angry with a vaporing creature like this. But I might as well get some information out of him.

"Tell me this," I asked; "if, for any reason, you should leave this place and throw up your situation, so to speak, would you have a successor?"

"You needn't think I am going," it said contemptuously. "None of your little tricks on me. But I'll just tell you, for your satisfaction, that if I should take it into my head to cut the place, there would be another ghost here in no time."

"What is it," I cried, stamping my foot, "that causes this house to be so haunted by ghosts, when there are hundreds and thousands of places where such apparitions are never seen?"

"Old fellow," said the spectre, folding its arms, and looking at me with half-shut eyes, "it isn't the house that draws the ghosts, it is somebody in it; and as long as you are here the place will be haunted. But you needn't mind that. Some houses have rats, some have fever-and-ague, and some have ghosts. Au revoir." And I was alone.

So then the spectral mortgage could never be lifted.

With heavy heart and feet I passed through the bosky grove to my once happy home.

I had not been there half an hour when Belle arrived. She had come by the morning train, and had nothing with her but a little hand-bag. I looked at her in astonishment.

"Infatuated girl," I cried, "could you not stay away from here three days?"

"I am glad you said that," she answered, taking a seat; "for now I think I am right in suspecting what was on your mind. I ran away from Madeline to see if I could find out what was at the bottom of this dreadful trouble between you. She told me what you said, and I don't believe you ever used those words to Pegram. And now I want to ask you one question. Had I, in any way, any thing to do with this?"

"No," said I, "not directly." And then emboldened by circumstances, I added: "But that secret visitor or friend of yours had much to do with it."

"I thought that might be so," she answered; "and now, George, I want to tell you something, I am afraid it will shock you very much."

"I have had so much to shock me lately that I can stand almost any thing now."

"Well then, it is this," she said. "That person whom I saw sometimes, and whom you once found under my window, is a ghost."

"Did you know that?" I cried. "I knew it was a ghost, but did not imagine that you had any suspicion of it."

"Why, yes," she answered, "I saw through him

almost from the very first. I was a good deal startled, and a little frightened when I found it out; but I soon felt that this ghost couldn't do me any harm, and you don't know how amusing it was. I always had a fancy for ghosts, but I never expected to meet with one like this."

"And so you knew all the time it wasn't a real man," I exclaimed, still filled with astonishment at what I had heard.

"A real man!" cried Belle, with considerable contempt in her tones. "Do you suppose I would become acquainted in that way with a real man, and let him come under my window and talk to me? I was determined not to tell any of you about it; for I knew you wouldn't approve of it, and would break up the fun some way. Now I wish most heartily that I had spoken of it."

"Yes," I answered, "it might have saved much trouble."

"But, oh! George," she continued, "you've no idea how funny it was! Such a ridiculous, self-conceited, old-fashioned ghost of a beau!"

"Yes." said I, "when it was alive it courted your grandmother."

"The impudence!" exclaimed Belle. "And to think that it supposed that I imagined it to be a real man! Why, one day, when it was talking to me it stepped back into a rose-bush; and it stood there ever so long, all mixed up with the roses and leaves."

"And you knew it all the time?"

These words were spoken in a hollow voice by some

one near us. Turning quickly, we saw the ghost of
Buck Edwards, but no longer the jaunty spectre we
had seen before. His hat was on the back of his head,
his knees were turned inward, his shoulders drooped,
his head hung, and his arms dangled limp at his sides.

"Yes," said Belle, "I knew it all the time."

The ghost looked at her with a faded, misty eye;
and then, instead of vanishing briskly as was his wont,
he began slowly and irresolutely to disappear. First
his body faded from view, then his head, leaving his
hat and boots. These gradually vanished, and the
last thing we saw of the once Buck Edwards was a
dissolving view of the tip-end of a limp and drooping
riding-whip.

"He is gone," said Belle. "We'll never see him
again."

"Yes," said I, "he is gone. I think your discovery of his real nature has completely broken up
that proud spirit. And now, what is to be done about
Madeline?"

"Wasn't it the ghost you called an interloper?"
asked Belle.

"Certainly it was," I replied.

"Well, then, go and tell her so," said Belle.

"About the ghost and all!" I exclaimed.

"Certainly," said she.

And together we went to Madeline, and I told her
all. I found her with her anger gone, and steeped in
misery. When I had finished, all Pegramed as she
was, she plunged into my arms. I pressed my wife
and child closely to my bosom, and we wept with joy.

When Will Crenshaw came home and was told this story, he said it didn't trouble him a bit.

" I'm not afraid of a rival like that," he remarked. " Such a suitor wouldn't stand a ghost of a chance."

" But I can tell you," said Madeline, " that you had better be up and doing on your own account. A girl like Belle needn't be expected to depend on the chance of a ghost."

Crenshaw heeded her words, and the young couple were married in the fall. The wedding took place in the little church near our house. It was a quiet marriage, and was attended by a strictly family party. At the conclusion of the ceremonies I felt, or saw, for I am sure I did not hear — a little sigh quite near me.

I turned, and sitting on the chancel-steps I saw the spectre of Buck Edwards. His head was bowed, and his hands, holding his hat and riding-whip, rested carelessly on his knees.

"Bedad, sir!" he exclaimed, "to think of it! If I hadn't cut up as I did I might have married, and have been that girl's grandfather!"

The idea made me smile.

"It can't be remedied now," I answered.

"Such a remark to make at a wedding!" said Madeline, giving me a punch with her reproachful elbow.

OUR ARCHERY CLUB.

WHEN an archery club was formed in our village,
I was among the first to join it; but I should
not, on this account, claim any extraordinary enthusiasm on the subject of archery, for nearly all the ladies
and gentlemen of the place were also among the first
to join.

Few of us, I think, had a correct idea of the popularity of archery in our midst, until the subject of a
club was broached. Then we all perceived what a
strong interest we felt in the study and use of the bow
and arrow. The club was formed immediately; and
our thirty members began to discuss the relative merits
of lancewood, yew, and greenheart bows, and to sur-
vey yards and lawns for suitable spots for setting up
targets for home practice.

Our weekly meetings, at which we came together to
show in friendly contest how much our home practice
had taught us, were held upon the village green, or
rather upon what had been intended to be the village
green. This pretty piece of ground, partly in smooth
lawn, and partly shaded by fine trees, was the property

of a gentleman of the place, who had presented it, under certain conditions, to the township. But as the township had never fulfilled any of the conditions, and had done nothing toward the improvement of the spot, further than to make it a grazing-place for local cows and goats, the owner had withdrawn his gift, shut out the cows and goats by a picket-fence, and having locked the gate, had hung up the key in his barn. When our club was formed, the green, as it was still called, was offered to us for our meetings; and with proper gratitude, we elected its owner to be our president.

This gentleman was eminently qualified for the presidency of an archery club. In the first place, he did not shoot: this gave him time and opportunity to attend to the shooting of others. He was a tall and pleasant man, a little elderly. This " elderliness," if I may so put it, seemed, in his case, to resemble some mild disorder, like a gentle rheumatism, which, while it prevented him from indulging in all the wild hilarities of youth, gave him, in compensation, a position, as one entitled to a certain consideration, which was very agreeable to him. His little disease was chronic, it is true, and it was growing upon him; but it was, so far, a pleasant ailment.

And so, with as much interest in bows, and arrows, and targets, and successful shots as any of us, he never fitted an arrow to a string, nor drew a bow; but he attended every meeting, settling disputed points (for he studied all the books on archery); encouraging the disheartened; holding back the eager ones, who would run to the targets as soon as they had shot. regardless of the fact that others were still shooting, and that the human body is not arrow-proof; and shedding about him that general aid and comfort which emanates from a good fellow, no matter what he may say or do.

There were persons — outsiders — who said that archery clubs always selected ladies for their presiding officers, but we did not care to be too much bound down and trammelled by customs and traditions. Another club might not have among its members such a genial, elderly gentleman, who owned a village green.

I soon found myself greatly interested in archery, especially when I succeeded in planting an arrow somewhere within the periphery of the target; but I never became such an enthusiast in bow-shooting as my friend Pepton.

If Pepton could have arranged matters to suit himself, he would have been born an archer; but as this did not happen to have been the case, he employed every means in his power to rectify what he considered this serious error in his construction. He gave his whole soul, and the greater part of his spare time, to archery; and as he was a young man of energy, this helped him along wonderfully.

His equipments were perfect: no one could excel him in this respect. His bow was snake-wood, backed with hickory. He carefully rubbed it down every evening with oil and bees-wax, and it took its repose in a green baize bag. His arrows were Philip Highfield's best; his strings the finest Flander's hemp.

He had shooting-gloves ; and he had little leathern tips, that could be screwed fast on the ends of what he called his string-fingers. He had a quiver and a belt ; and when equipped for the weekly meetings, he carried a fancy-colored wiping-tassel, and a little ebony grease-pot, hanging from his belt. He wore, when shooting, a polished arm-guard or bracer ; and if he had heard of any thing else that an archer should have, he straightway would have procured it.

Pepton was a single man ; and he lived with two good old maiden ladies, who took as much care of him as if they had been his mothers. And he was such a good, kind fellow that he deserved all the attention they gave him. They felt a great interest in his archery pursuits, and shared his anxious solicitude in the selection of a suitable place to hang his bow.

"You see," said he, "a fine bow like this, when not in use, should always be in a perfectly dry place."

"And when in use, too," said Miss Martha ; "for I am sure that you oughtn't to be standing and shooting in any damp spot. There's no surer way of gettin' chilled."

To which sentiment Miss Maria agreed, and suggested wearing rubber shoes, or having a board to stand on, when the club met after a rain.

Pepton first hung his bow in the hall ; but after he had arranged it symmetrically upon two long nails (bound with green worsted, lest they should scratch the bow through its woollen cover), he reflected that the front door would frequently be open, and that damp draughts must often go through the hall. He

was sorry to give up this place for his bow, for it was
convenient and appropriate; and for an instant he
thought that it might remain, if the front door could
be kept shut, and visitors admitted through a little
side door, which the family generally used, and which
was almost as convenient as the other, — except, indeed, on wash-days, when a wet sheet or some article
of wearing apparel was apt to be hung in front of it.
But, although wash-day occurred but once a week,
and although it was comparatively easy, after a little
practice, to bob under a high-propped sheet, Pepton's
heart was too kind to allow his mind to dwell upon
this plan.   So he drew the nails from the wall of the
hall, and put them up in various places about the
house.   His own room had to be aired a great deal in
all weathers, and so that would not do at all.   The
wall above the kitchen fire-place would be a good loca-
tion, for the chimney was nearly always warm; but
Pepton could not bring himself to keep his bow in the
kitchen: there would be nothing æsthetic about such
a disposition of it; and, besides, the girl might be
tempted to string and bend it.   The old ladies really
did not want it in the parlor, for its length and its
green baize cover would make it an encroaching and
unbecoming neighbor to the little engravings and the
big samplers, the picture-frames of acorns and pine-
cones, the fancifully patterned ornaments of clean
wheat-straw, and all the quaint adornments which had
hung upon those walls for so many years.   But they
did not say so.   If it had been necessary, to make
room for the bow, they would have taken down the

pencilled profiles of their grandfather, their grandmother, and their father when a little boy, which hung
in a row over the mantel-piece.

However, Pepton did not ask this sacrifice. In the
summer evenings, the parlor windows must be open.
The dining-room was really very little used in the
evening, except when Miss Maria had stockings to
darn ; and then she always sat in that apartment, and
of course she had the windows open. But Miss Maria
was very willing to bring her work into the parlor, —
it was foolish, any way, to have a feeling about darn-
ing stockings before chance company, — and then the
dining-room could be kept shut up after tea. So into
the wall of that neat little room Pepton drove his
worsted-covered nails, and on them carefully laid his
bow. And the next day Miss Martha and Miss Maria
went about the house, and covered the nail-holes he
had made with bits of wall-paper, carefully snipped
out to fit the patterns, and pasted on so neatly that no
one would have suspected they were there.

One afternoon, as I was passing the old ladies'
house, I saw, or thought I saw, two men carrying in a
coffin. I was struck with alarm.

"What!" I thought, "can either of those good
women? —— Or, can Pepton?" ——

Without a moment's hesitation, I rushed in behind
the men. There, at the foot of the stairs, directing
them, stood Pepton. Then it was not he! I seized
him sympathetically by the hand.

"Which?" —— I faltered. "Which? Who is
that coffin for?"

"Coffin!" cried Pepton, "why, my dear fellow, that is not a coffin. That is my ascham."

"Ascham?" I exclaimed. What is that?"

"Come and look at it," he said. when the men had set it on end against the wall; "it is an upright closet, or receptacle for an archer's armament. Here is a place to stand the bow; here are supports for the arrows and quivers; here are shelves and hooks, on which to lay or hang every thing the merry man can need. And you see, moreover, that it is lined with green plush, and that the door fits tightly, so that it can stand anywhere, and there need be no fear of draughts or dampness affecting my bow. Isn't it a perfect thing? You ought to get one."

I admitted the perfection, but agreed no further. I had not the income of my good Pepton.

Pepton was, indeed, most wonderfully well equipped, and yet, little did those dear old ladies think, when they carefully dusted and reverentially gazed at the bunches of arrows, the arm-bracers, the gloves, the grease-pots, and all the rest of the paraphernalia of archery, as it hung around Pepton's room; or when they afterward allowed a particular friend to peep at it, all arranged so orderly within the ascham; or when they looked with sympathetic, loving admiration on the beautiful polished bow, when it was taken out of its bag, — little did they think. I say, that Pepton was the very poorest shot in the club. In all the surface of the much perforated targets of the club, there was scarcely a hole that he could put his hand upon his heart and say he made.

Indeed, I think it was the truth that Pepton was born not to be an archer. There were young fellows in the club, who shot with bows that cost no more than Pepton's tassels, but who could stand up and whang arrows into the targets all the afternoon, if they could get a chance; and there were ladies who made hits five times out of six; and there were also all the grades of archers common to any club. But there was no one but himself in Pepton's grade. He stood alone, and it was never any trouble to add up his score.

And yet he was not discouraged. He practised every day except Sundays, and indeed he was the only person in the club who practised at night. When he told me about this, I was a little surprised.

"Why, it's easy enough," said he. "You see, I hung a lantern, with a reflector, before the target, just a little to one side. It lighted up the target beautifully; and I believe there was a better chance of hitting it than by daylight, for the only thing you could see was the target, and so your attention was not distracted. To be sure," he said, in answer to a question, "it was a good deal of trouble to find the arrows, but that I always have. When I get so expert that I can put all the arrows into the target, there will be no trouble of the kind, night or day. However," he continued, "I don't practise any more by night. The other evening I sent an arrow slam-bang into the lantern, and broke it all to flinders. Borrowed lantern, too. Besides, I found it made Miss Martha very nervous to have me shooting about the house after dark. She had a friend, who had a little boy, who was hit in the leg by an arrow from a bow, which, she says, accidentally went off in the night, of its own accord. She is certainly a little mixed in her mind in regard to this matter: but I wished to respect her feelings, and so shall not use another lantern.''

As I have said, there were many good archers among the ladies of our club. Some of them, after we had been organized for a month or two, made scores that few of the gentlemen could excel. But the lady who attracted the greatest attention when she shot was Miss Rosa.

When this very pretty young lady stood up before the ladies' target — her left side well advanced, her bow firmly held out in her strong left arm, which never quivered, her head a little bent to the right, her arrow drawn back by three well-gloved fingers to the tip of her little ear, her dark eyes steadily fixed upon the gold, and her dress — well fitted over her fine and vigorous figure — falling in graceful folds about her feet, we all stopped shooting to look at her.

'' There is something statuesque about her,'' said Pepton, who ardently admired her, '' and yet there isn't. A statue could never equal her unless we knew there was a probability of movement in it. And the only statues which have that are the Jarley wax-works, which she does not resemble in the least. There is only one thing that that girl needs to make her a perfect archer, and that is to be able to aim better.''

This was true. Miss Rosa did need to aim better. Her arrows had a curious habit of going on all sides of the target, and it was very seldom that one chanced to stick into it. For, if she did make a hit, we all knew it was chance and that there was no probability of her doing it again. Once she put an arrow right into the centre of the gold, — one of the finest shots ever made on the ground, — but she didn't hit the target again for two weeks. She was almost as bad a shot as Pepton, and that is saying a good deal.

One evening I was sitting with Pepton on the little front porch of the old ladies' house, where we were taking our after-dinner smoke while Miss Martha and Miss Maria were washing, with their own white hands, the china and glass in which they took so much pride. I often used to come over and spend an hour with Pepton. He liked to have some one to whom he could talk on the subjects which filled his soul, and I liked to hear him talk.

"I tell you," said he, as he leaned back in his chair, with his feet carefully disposed on the railing so that they would not injure Miss Maria's Madeira vine, " I tell you, sir, that there are two things I crave with all my power of craving; two goals I fain would reach; two diadems I would wear upon my brow. One of these is to kill an eagle — or some large bird — with a shaft from my good bow. I would then have it stuffed and mounted, with the very arrow that killed it still sticking in its breast. This trophy of my skill I would have fastened against the wall of my room, or my hall, and I would feel proud to think that my grandchildren could point to that bird — which I would carefully bequeath to my descendants — and say, 'My grand'ther shot that bird, and with that very arrow.' Would it not stir your pulses, if you could do a thing like that?"

" I should have to stir them up a good deal before I could do it," I replied. " It would be a hard thing to shoot an eagle with an arrow. If you want a stuffed bird to bequeath, you'd better use a rifle."

" A rifle!" exclaimed Pepton. "There would be no glory in that. There are lots of birds shot with rifles, — eagles, hawks, wild geese, tom-tits " ——

" Oh, no!" I interrupted, " not tom-tits."

" Well, perhaps they are too little for a rifle," said he; " but what I mean to say is, that I wouldn't care at all for an eagle I had shot with a rifle. You couldn't show the ball that killed him. If it were put in properly, it would be inside, where it couldn't be seen. No, sir; it is ever so much more honorable, and far more difficult, too, to hit an eagle than to hit a target."

" That is very true," I answered, " especially in these days, when there are so few eagles and so many targets. But what is your other diadem?"

" That," said Pepton, " is to see Miss Rosa wear the badge."

" Indeed!" said I; and from that moment I began to understand Pepton's hopes in regard to the grandmother of those children who should point to the eagle.

" Yes, sir," he continued, " I should be truly happy to see her win the badge. And she ought to win it. No one shoots more correctly, and with a better understanding of all the rules, than she does. There must, truly, be something the matter with her aiming. I've half a mind to coach her a little."

I turned aside to see who was coming down the road. I would not have had him know I smiled.

The most objectionable person in our club was O. J. Hollingsworth. He was a good enough fellow in himself, but it was as an archer that we objected to him. There was, so far as I know, scarcely a rule of archery that he did not habitually violate. Our president and nearly all of us remonstrated with him, and Pepton even went to see him on the subject; but it was all to no purpose. With a quiet disregard of other people's ideas about bow-shooting and other people's opinions about himself, he persevered in a style of shooting which appeared absolutely absurd to any one who knew any thing of the rules and methods of archery.

I used to like to look at him when his turn came around to shoot. He was not such a pleasing object of vision as Miss Rosa, but his style was so entirely novel to me that it was interesting. He held the bow horizontally, instead of perpendicularly, like other archers; and he held it well down — about opposite his waistband. He did not draw his arrow back to his ear, but he drew it back to the lower button of his vest. Instead of standing upright, with his left side to the target, he faced it full, and leaned forward over his arrow, in an attitude which reminded me of a Roman soldier about to fall upon his sword. When he had seized the nock of his arrow between his finger and thumb, he languidly glanced at the target, raised his bow a little, and let fly. The provoking thing about it was that he nearly always hit. If he had only known how to stand, and hold his bow, and draw back his arrow, he would have been a very good archer. But, as it was, we could not help laughing at him, although our president always discountenanced any thing of the kind.

Our Champion was a tall man, very cool and steady, who went to work at archery exactly as if he were paid a salary, and intended to earn his money honestly. He did the best he could in every way. He generally shot with one of the bows owned by the club; but if any one on the ground had a better one, he would borrow it. He used to shoot sometimes with Pepton's bow, which he declared to be a most capital one; but as Pepton was always very nervous when he saw his bow in the hands of another than himself, the Champion soon ceased to borrow it.

. There were two badges, one of green silk and gold, for the ladies, and one of green and red, for the gentlemen; and these were shot for at each weekly meeting. With the exception of a few times, when the club was first formed, the Champion had always worn the gentlemen's badge. Many of us tried hard to win it from him; but we never could succeed — he shot too well.

On the morning of one of our meeting days, the Champion told me, as I was going to the city with him, that he would not be able to return at his usual hour that afternoon. He would be very busy, and would have to wait for the 6.15 train, which would bring him home too late for the archery meeting. So he gave me the badge, asking me to hand it to the president.

that he might bestow it on the successful competitor that afternoon.

We were all rather glad that the Champion was obliged to be absent. Here was a chance for some one of us to win the badge. It was not, indeed, an opportunity for us to win a great deal of honor, for if the Champion were to be there, we should have no chance at all; but we were satisfied with this much, having no reason — in the present, at least — to expect any thing more.

So we went to the targets with a new zeal, and most of us shot better than we had ever shot before. In this number was O. J. Hollingsworth. He excelled himself, and, what was worse, he excelled all the rest of us. He actually made a score of eighty-five in twenty-four shots, which at that time was remarkably good shooting, for our club. This was dreadful! To have a fellow, who didn't know how to shoot, beat us all, was too bad. If any visitor who knew any thing at all of archery should see that the member who wore the champion's badge was a man who held his bow as if he had the stomach-ache, it would ruin our character as a club. It was not to be borne.

Pepton, in particular, felt greatly outraged. We had met very promptly that afternoon, and had finished our regular shooting much earlier than usual; and now a knot of us were gathered together, talking over this unfortunate occurrence.

" I don't intend to stand it," Pepton suddenly exclaimed. " I feel it as a personal disgrace. I'm going to have the Champion here before dark. By the

rules, he has a right to shoot until the president de-
clares it is too late. Some of you fellows stay here,
and I'll bring him.''

And away he ran, first giving me charge of his pre-
cious bow. There was no need of his asking us to
stay. We were bound to see the fun out; and to fill
up the time our president offered a special prize of a
handsome bouquet from his gardens, to be shot for by
the ladies.

Pepton ran to the railroad station, and telegraphed
to the Champion. This was his message :

"You are absolutely needed here. If possible, take the 5.30
train for Ackford. I will drive over for you. Answer."

There was no train before the 6.15 by which the
Champion could come directly to our village ; but
Ackford, a small town about three miles distant, was
on another railroad, on which there were frequent afternoon trains.

The Champion answered :

"All right. Meet me."

Then Pepton rushed to our livery stable, hired a
horse and buggy, and drove to Ackford.

A little after half-past six, when several of us were
beginning to think that Pepton had failed in his plans,
he drove rapidly into the grounds, making a very short
turn at the gate, and pulled up his panting horse just
in time to avoid running over three ladies, who were
seated on the grass. The Champion was by his side !

The latter lost no time in talking or salutations.
He knew what he had been brought there to do, and

he immediately set about trying to do it. He took Pepton's bow, which the latter urged upon him; he stood up, straight and firm on the line, at thirty-five yards from the gentlemen's target; he carefully selected his arrows, examining the feathers and wiping away any bit of soil that might be adhering to the points after some one had shot them into the turf; with vigorous arm he drew each arrow to its head; he fixed his eyes and his whole mind on the centre of the target; he shot his twenty-four arrows, handed to him, one by one, by Pepton, and he made a score of ninety-one.

The whole club had been scoring the shots, as they were made, and when the last arrow plumped into the red ring, a cheer arose from every member excepting three: the Champion, the president and O. J. Hollingsworth. But Pepton cheered loudly enough to make up these deficiencies.

"What in the mischief did they cheer him for?" asked Hollingsworth of me. "They didn't cheer me, when I beat everybody on the gounds, an hour ago. And it's no new thing for him to win the badge; he does it every time."

"Well," said I, frankly, "I think the club, *as a club*, objects to your wearing the badge, because you don't know how to shoot."

"Don't know how to shoot!" he cried. "Why, I can hit the target better than any of you. Isn't that what you try to do when you shoot?"

"Yes," said I, "of course that is what we try to do. But we try to do it in the proper way."

" Proper grandmother ! " he exclaimed. " It don't seem to help you much. The best thing you fellows can do is to learn to shoot my way, and then perhaps you may be able to hit oftener."

When the Champion had finished shooting, he went home to his dinner, but many of us stood about, talking over our great escape.

" I feel as if I had done that myself," said Pepton. " I am almost as proud as if I had shot — well, not an eagle, but a soaring lark."

" Why, that ought to make you prouder than the other," said I ; " for a lark, especially when it's soaring, must be a good deal harder to hit than an eagle."

" That's so," said Pepton, reflectively ; " but I'll stick to the lark. I'm proud."

During the next month our style of archery improved very much, so much, indeed, that we increased our distance, for gentlemen, to forty yards, and that for ladies to thirty, and also had serious thoughts of challenging the Ackford club to a match. But as this was generally understood to be a crack club, we finally determined to defer our challenge until the next season.

When I say we improved, I do not mean all of us. I do not mean Miss Rosa. Although her attitudes were as fine as ever, and every motion as true to rule as ever, she seldom made a hit. Pepton actually did try to teach her how to aim ; but the various methods of pointing the arrow which he suggested resulted in such wild shooting, that the boys who picked up the arrows never dared to stick the points of their noses beyond their boarded barricade, during Miss Rosa's turns at the target. But she was not discouraged; and Pepton often assured her that if she would keep up a good heart, and practise regularly, she would get the badge yet. As a rule, Pepton was so honest and truthful that a little statement of this kind, especially under the circumstances, might be forgiven him.

One day Pepton came to me and announced that he had made a discovery.

"It's about archery," he said; "and I don't mind telling you, because I know you will not go about telling everybody else, and also because I want to see you succeed as an archer."

"I am very much obliged," I said; "and what is the discovery?"

"It's this," he answered. "When you draw your bow, bring the nock of your arrow" — he was always very particular about technical terms — "well up to your ear. Having done that, don't bother any more about your right hand. It has nothing to do with the correct pointing of your arrow, for it must be kept close to your right ear, just as if it were screwed there. Then with your left hand bring around the bow so that your fist — with the arrow-head, which is resting on top of it — shall point, as nearly as you can make it, directly at the centre of the target. Then let fly, and ten to one you'll make a hit. Now, what do you think of that, for a discovery? I've thoroughly tested the plan, and it works splendidly."

"I think," said I, "that you have discovered the way in which good archers shoot. You have stated the correct method of managing a bow and arrow."

"Then you don't think it's an original method with me?"

"Certainly not," I answered.

"But it's the correct way?"

"There's no doubt of that," said I.

"Well," said Pepton, "then I shall make it my way."

He did so ; and the consequence was that one day, when the Champion happened to be away, Pepton won the badge. When the result was announced, we were all surprised, but none so much so as Pepton himself. He had been steadily improving since he had adopted a good style of shooting, but he had had no idea that he would that day be able to win the badge.

When our president pinned the emblem of success upon the lapel of his coat, Pepton turned pale, and then he flushed. He thanked the president, and was about to thank the ladies and gentlemen ; but probably recollecting that we had had nothing to do with it, — unless, indeed, we had shot badly on his behalf, — he refrained. He said little, but I could see that he was very proud and very happy. There was but one drawback to his triumph : Miss Rosa was not there. She was a very regular attendant, but for some reason she was absent on this momentous afternoon. I did not say any thing to him on the subject, but I knew he felt this absence deeply.

But this cloud could not wholly overshadow his happiness. He walked home alone, his face beaming, his eyes sparkling, and his good bow under his arm.

That evening I called on him ; for I thought that,

when he had cooled down a little, he would like to talk over the affair. But he was not in. Miss Maria said that he had gone out as soon as he had finished his dinner, which he hurried through in a way which would certainly injure his digestion if he kept up the practice ; and dinner was late, too, for they waited for him ; and the archery meeting lasted a long time to-day ; and it really was not right for him to stay out after the dew began to fall with only ordinary shoes on, for what's the good of knowing how to shoot a bow and arrow, if you're laid up in your bed with rheumatism or disease of the lungs ! Good old lady ! She would have kept Pepton in a green baize bag, had such a thing been possible.

The next morning, full two hours before church-time, Pepton called on me. His face was still beaming. I could not help smiling.

" Your happiness lasts well," I said.

" Lasts ! " he exclaimed. " Why shouldn't it last ! "

" There's no reason why it should not — at least for a week," I said. " And even longer, if you repeat your success."

I did not feel so much like congratulating Pepton as I had on the previous evening. I thought he was making too much of his badge-winning.

" Look here ! " said Pepton, seating himself, and drawing his chair close to me, " you are shooting wild — very wild indeed. You don't even see the target. Let me tell you something. Last evening I went to see Miss Rosa. She was delighted at my success. I had not expected this. I thought she would be pleased,

but not to such a degree. Her congratulations were
so warm that they set me on fire."

"They must have been very warm indeed," I remarked.

"' Miss Rosa,' said I," continued Pepton, without
regarding my interruption, "' it has been my fondest
hope to see you wear the badge.' 'But I never could
get it, you know,' she said. 'You have got it,' I exclaimed. 'Take this. I won it for you. Make me
happy by wearing it.' 'I can't do that,' she said.
'That is a gentleman's badge.' 'Take it,' I cried,
'gentleman and all!'

"I can't tell you all that happened after that," continued Pepton. "You know it wouldn't do. It is
enough to say that she wears the badge. And we are
both her own — the badge and I!"

Now I congratulated him in good earnest. There
was a reason for it.

"I don't care a snap now for shooting an eagle,"
said Pepton, springing to his feet, and striding up and
down the floor. "Let 'em all fly free for me. I have
made the most glorious shot that man could make. I
have hit the gold — hit it fair in the very centre! And
what's more, I've knocked it clean out of the target!
Nobody else can ever make such a shot. The rest
of you fellows will have to be content to hit the
red, the blue, the black, or the white. The gold is
mine!"

I called on the old ladies, some time after this, and
found them alone. They were generally alone in the
evenings now. We talked about Pepton's engagement,

and I found them resigned. They were sorry to lose him, but they wanted him to be happy.

"We have always known," said Miss Martha, with a little sigh, "that we must die, and that he must get married. But we don't intend to repine. These things will come to people." And her little sigh was followed by a smile, still smaller.

THAT SAME OLD 'COON.

WE were sitting on the store-porch of a small Virginia village. I was one of the party, and Martin Heiskill was the other one. Martin had been out fishing, which was an unusual thing for him.

"Yes, sir," said he, as he held up the small string of fish which he had laid carefully under his chair when he sat down to light his pipe; "that's all I've got to show for a day's work. But 'taint often that I waste time that way. I don't b'lieve in huntin' fur a thing that ye can't see. If fishes sot on trees, now, and ye could shoot at 'em, I'd go out and hunt fishes with anybody. But its mighty triflin' work to be goin' it blind in a mill-pond."

I ventured to state that there were fish that were occasionally found on trees. In India, for instance, a certain fish climbs trees.

"A which what's?" exclaimed Martin, with an arrangement of pronouns peculiar to himself.

"Oh, yes!" he said, when I had told him all I knew about this bit of natural history. "That's very likely. I reckon they do that up North, where you come from, in some of them towns you was tellin' me about, where there's so many houses that they tech each other."

" That's all true about the fishes, Martin," said I, wisely making no reference to the houses, for I did not want to push his belief too hard ; " but we'll drop them now."

" Yes," said he, " I think we'd better."

Martin was a good fellow and no fool ; but he had not travelled much, and had no correct ideas of cities, nor, indeed, of much of any thing outside of his native backwoods. But of those backwoods he knew more than any other man I ever met. He liked to talk, but he resented tall stories.

" Martin," said I, glad to change the subject, " do you think there'll be many 'coons about, this fall?"

" About as many as common, I reckon," he answered. " What do you want to know fur?"

" I'd like to go out 'coon-hunting," I said ; " that's something I have never tried."

" Well," said he, " I don't s'pose your goin' will make much difference in the number of 'em, but, what's the good uv it? You'd better go 'possum-huntin'. You kin eat a 'possum."

" Don't you ever eat 'coons?" I asked.

" Eat 'coons!" he exclaimed, with contempt. " Why, there isn't a nigger in this county'd eat a 'coon. They aint fit to eat."

" I should think they'd be as good as 'possums," said I. " They feed on pretty much the same things, don't they?"

" Well, there aint much difference, that way ; but a

'possum's a mighty different thing from a 'coon, when ye come to eat him. A 'possum's more like a kind o' tree-pig. An' when he's cooked, he's sweeter than any suckin'-pig you ever see. But a 'coon's more like a cat. Who'd eat cats?"

I was about to relate some city sausage stories, but I refrained.

"To be sure," continued Martin, "there's Col. Tibbs, who says he's eat 'coon-meat, and liked it fust-rate; but then ag'in, he says frogs is good to eat, so ye see there's no dependin' on what people say. Now, I know what I'm a-talkin' about; 'coons aint fit fur human bein's to eat."

'What makes you hunt 'em, then?" I asked.

"Hunt 'em fur fun," said the old fellow, striking a lucifer match under his chair, to re-light his pipe. "Ef ye talk about vittles, that's one thing; an' ef ye talk about fun, that's another thing. An' I don't know now whether you'd think it was fun. I kinder think you wouldn't. I reckon it'd seem like pretty hard work to you."

"I suppose it would," I said; "there are many things that would be hard work to me, that would be nothing but sport to an old hunter like you."

"You're right, there, sir. You never spoke truer than that in your life. There's no man inside o' six counties that's hunted more'n I have. I've been at it ever sence I was a youngster; an' I've got a lot o' fun out uv it, — more fun than any thing else, fur that matter. You see, afore the war, people used to go huntin' more for real sport than they do now. An'

'twa'n't because there was more game in this country
then than there is now, fur there wa'n't, — not half as
much. There's more game in Virginny now than
there's been any time this fifty years."

I expressed my surprise at this statement, and he
continued :

" It all stands to reason, plain enough. Ef you
don't kill them wild critters off, they'll jist breed and
breed, till the whole country gits full uv 'em. An'
nobody had no time to hunt 'em durin' the war, — we
was busy huntin' different game then, and sometimes
we was hunted ourselves; an' since then the most uv
us has had to knuckle down to work, — no time for
huntin' when you've got to do your own hoein' and
ploughin', — or, at least, a big part uv it. An' I tell
ye that back there in the mountains there's lots o' deer
where nobody livin' about here ever saw 'em before,
and as fur turkeys, and 'coons, and 'possums, there's
more an' more uv' em ev'ry year, but as fur beavers, —
them confounded chills-and-fever rep-tyles, — there's
jist millions uv 'em, more or less."

" Do beavers have chills and fever? " I asked won-
deringly.

" No," said he, " I wish they did. But they give it
to folks. There aint nothin' on earth that's raised the
price o' quinine in this country like them beavers. Ye
see, they've jist had the'r own way now, pretty much
ever sence the war broke out, and they've gone to
work and built dams across pretty nigh all the cricks
we got, and that floods the bottom-lands, uv course,
and makes ma'shes and swamps, where they used to

be fust-rate corn-land. Why, I tell ye, sir, down here on Colt's Creek there's a beaver-dam a quarter uv a mile long, an' the water's backed up all over every thing. Aint that enough to give a whole county the chills? An' it does it too. Ef the people'd all go and sit on that there dam, they'd shake it down. I tell ye, sir, the war give us, in this country, a good many things we didn't want, and among 'em's chills. Before the war, nobody never heard of sich things as chills round about hyar. 'Taint on'y the beavers, nuther. When ye can't afford to hire more'n three or four niggers to work a big farm, 'taint likely ye kin do no ditchin', and all the branches and the ditches in the bottom-lands fills up, an' a feller's best corn-fields is pretty much all swamp, and his family has to live on quinine."

"I should think it would pay well to hunt and trap these beavers," I remarked.

"Well, so it does, sometimes," said Martin ; "but half the people aint got no time. Now it's different with me, because I'm not a-farmin'. An' then it aint everybody that kin git 'em. It takes a kind o' eddica-tion to hunt beaver. But you was a-askin' about 'coons."

"Yes," I said. "I'd like to go 'coon-hunting."

"There's lots o' fun in it," said he, knocking the ashes out of his pipe, and putting up his cowhide boots on the top of the porch-railing in front of him.

"About two or three years afore the war, I went out on a 'coon-hunt, which was the liveliest hunt I ever see in all my life. I never had sich a good hunt

afore, nur never sence. I was a-livin' over in Pow-
hattan, and the 'coon was Haskinses 'coon. They
called him Haskinses 'coon, because he was 'most
allus seen somewhere on ole Tom Haskinses farm.
Tom's dead now, an' so is the 'coon ; but the farm's
thar, an' I'm here, so ye kin b'lieve this story, jist as
ef it was printed on paper. It was the most confound-
edest queer 'coon anybody ever see in all this whole
world. An' the queerness was this : it hadn't no
stripes to its tail. Now ye needn't say to me that
no 'coon was ever that way, fur this 'coon was, an' that
settles it. All 'coons has four or five brown stripes
a-runnin' roun' their tails, — all 'cept this one 'coon
uv Haskinses. An' what's more, this was the sava-
gest 'coon anybody ever did see in this whole world.
That's what sot everybody huntin' him ; fur the sav-
ager a coon is, an' the more grit ther' is in him. the
more's the fun when he comes to fight the dogs — fur
that's whar the fun comes in. An' ther' is 'coons as
kin lick a whole pack o' dogs, an' git off ; and this is
jist what Haskinses 'coon did, lots o' times. I b'lieve
every nigger in the county, an' pretty much half the
white men, had been out huntin' that 'coon, and they'd
never got him yit. Ye see he was so derned cunnin'
an' gritty, that when ye cut his tree down, he'd jist
go through the dogs like a wasp in a Sunday school,
an' git away, as I tell ye. He must a' had teeth more'n
an inch long, and he had a mighty tough bite to him.
Quick, too, as a black-snake. Well, they never got
him, no how ; but he was often seed, fur he'd even let
a feller as hadn't a gun with him git a look at him in

the day-time, which is contrary to the natur' of a 'coon,
which keeps dark all day an on'y comes out arter dark.
But this here 'coon o' Haskinses was different from
any 'coon anybody ever see in all this world. Sometimes ye'd see him a-settin' down by a branch, a-dip-
pin' his food inter the water every time he took a bite,
which is the natur' of a coon; but if ye put yer hand
inter yer pocket fur so much as a pocket-pistol, he'd
skoot afore ye could wink.

  "Well, I made up my mind I'd go out after Haskinses 'coon, and I got up a huntin' party. 'Twa'n't
no trouble to do that. In them days ye could git up
a huntin' party easier than any thing else in this whole
world. All ye had to do was to let the people know,
an' they'd be thar, black an' white. Why, I tell ye,
sir. they used to go fox-huntin' a lot in them days, an'
there wasn't half as many foxes as ther' is now,
nuther. If a feller woke up bright an' early, an' felt
like fox-huntin', all he had to do was to git on his
horse, and take his dogs and his horn, and ride off to
his nex' neighbor's, an' holler. An' up'd jump the
nex' feller, and git on his horse, and take his dogs,
and them two'd ride off to the nex' farm an' holler,
an' keep that up till ther' was a lot uv 'em, with the'r
hounds, and away they'd go, tip-it-ty-crack, after the
fox an' the hounds — fur it didn't take long for them
dogs to scar' up a fox. An' they'd keep it up, too,
like good fellers. Ther' was a party uv 'em, once,
started out of a Friday mornin', and the'r fox, which
was a red fox (fur a gray fox aint no good fur a long
run) took 'em clean over into Albemarle, and none uv

'em didn't get back home till arter dark, Saturday. That was the way we used to hunt.

"Well, I got up my party, and we went out arter Haskinses 'coon. We started out pretty soon arter supper. Ole Tom Haskins himself was along, because, uv course, he wanted to see his 'coon killed; an' ther' was a lot of other fellers that you wouldn't know ef I was to tell ye the'r names. Ye see, it was 'way down at the lower end of the county that I was a-livin' then. An' ther' was about a dozen niggers with axes, an' five or six little black boys to carry light-wood. There was no less than thirteen dogs, all 'coon-hunters.

"Ye see, the 'coon-dog is sometimes a hound, an' sometimes he isn't. It takes a right smart dog to hunt a 'coon; and sometimes ye kin train a dog, thet aint a reg'lar huntin'-dog, to be a fust-rate 'coon-dog, pertickerlerly when the fightin' comes in. To be sure, ye want a dog with a good nose to him to foller up a 'coon; but ye want fellers with good jaws and teeth, and plenty of grit, too. We had thirteen of the best 'coon-dogs in the whole world, an' that was enough fur any one 'coon, I say; though Haskinses 'coon was a pertickerler kind of a 'coon, as I tell ye.

"Pretty soon arter we got inter Haskinses oak woods, jist back o' the house, the dogs got on the track uv a 'coon, an' after 'em we all went, as hard as we could skoot. Uv course we didn't know that it was Haskinses 'coon we was arter; but we made up our minds, afore we started, thet when we killed a 'coon and found it wasn't Haskinses 'coon, we'd jist keep on till we did find him. We didn't 'spect to

have much trouble a-findin' him, fur we know'd pretty
much whar he lived, and we went right thar. Taint
often anybody hunts fur one pertickerler 'coon ; but
that was the matter this time, as I tell ye.''

It was evident from the business-like way in which
Martin Heiskill started into this story, that he wouldn't
get home in time to have his fish cooked for supper,
but that was not my affair. It was not every day that
the old fellow chose to talk, and I was glad enough to
have him go on as long as he would.

"As I tell ye,'' continued Martin, looking steadily
over the toe of one of his boots, as if taking a long
aim at some distant turkey, "we put off, hot and
heavy, arter that ar 'coon, and hard work it was too.
The dogs took us down through the very stickeryest
part of the woods, and then down the holler by the
edge of Lumley's mill-pond, — whar no human bein'
in this world ever walked or run afore, I truly b'lieve,
fur it was the meanest travellin' groun' I ever see, — and
then back inter the woods ag'in. But 'twa'n't long afore
we came up to the dogs a-barkin' and howlin' around
a big chestnut-oak about three foot through, an' we
knew we had him. That is, ef it wa'n't Haskinses
'coon. Ef it was his 'coon, may be we had him, and
may be we hadn't. The boys lighted up their light-
wood torches, and two niggers with axes bent to work
at the tree. And them as wasn't choppin' had as
much as they could do to keep the dogs back out o'
the way o' the axes.

"The dogs they was jist goin' on as ef they was
mad, and ole Uncle Pete Williams — he was the one

thet was a-holdin' on to Chink, the big dog — that
dog's name was Chinkerpin, an' he was the best
'coon-dog in the whole world, I reckon. He was a
big hound, brown an' black, an' he was the on'y dog
in thet pack thet had never had a fight with Haskinses
'coon. They fetched him over from Cumberland,
a-purpose for this hunt. Well, as I tell ye, ole Pete,
says he, 'Thar aint no mistook dis time, Mahsr Tom,
now I tell you. Dese yar dogs knows well 'nuf dat
dat 'coon's Mahsr Tom's 'coon, an' dey tell Chink too,
fur he's a-doin' de debbil's own pullin' dis time.' An'
I reckon Uncle Pete was 'bout right, fur I thought the
dog ud pull him off his legs afore he got through.

" Pretty soon the niggers hollered fur to stan' from
under, an' down came the chestnut-oak with the big
smash, an' then ev'ry dog an' man an' nigger made
one skoot fur that tree. But they couldn't see no
'coon, fur he was in a hole 'bout half way up the
trunk ; an' then there was another high ole time keepin'
back the dogs till the fellers with axes cut him out.
It didn't take long to do that. The tree was a kind o'
rotten up thar. and afore I know'd it, out hopped the
'coon: and then in less then half a shake, there was
sich a fight as you never see in all this world.

" At first, it 'peared like it was a blamed mean
thing to let thirteen dogs fight one 'coon ; but pretty
soon I thought it was a little too bad to have on'y
thirteen dogs fur sich a fiery savage beast as that there
'coon was. He jist laid down on his back an' buzzed
around like a coffee-mill, an' whenever a dog got a
snap at him, he got the 'coon's teeth inter him quick

as lightnin'. Ther' was too many dogs in that fight, an' 'twa'n't long before some uv 'em found that out, and got out o' the muss. An' it was some o' the dogs thet had the best chance at the 'coon thet left fust.

"Afore long, though, old Chink, who'd a been a-watchin' his chance, he got a good grip on that 'coon, an' that was the end of him. He jist throw'd up his hand.

"The minute I seed the fight was over, I rushed in an' grabbed that 'coon, an' like to got grabbed myself, too, in doin' it, 'specially by Chink, who didn't know me. One o' the boys brought a light-wood torch so's we could see the little beast.

"Well, 'twa'n't Haskinses 'coon. He had rings round his tail, jist as reg'lar as ef he was the feller that set the fashion. So ther' was more 'coon-huntin' to be done that night. But ther' wa'n't nobody that objected to that, fur we were jist gittin' inter the fun o' the thing. An' I made up my mind I wasn't a-goin' home without the tail off er Haskinses 'coon.

"I disremember now whether the nex' thing we killed was a 'coon or a 'possum. It's a long time ago, and I've been on lots o' hunts since thet; but the main p'ints o' this hunt I aint likely to furgit, fur, as I tell ye, this was the liveliest 'coon-hunt I ever went out on.

"Ef it was a 'possum we got next, ther' wasn't much fun about it, fur a 'possum's not a game beast. Ther's no fight in him, though his meat's better. When ye tree a 'possum an' cut down the tree, an' cut him out uv his hole, ef he's in one, he jist keels over an' makes b'lieve he's dead, though that's jinerally no use

at all, fur he's real dead in a minute, and it's hardly
wuth while fur him to take the trouble uv puttin' on
the sham. Sometimes a 'possum'll hang by his tail
to the limb of a tree, an' ye kin knock him down without cuttin' the tree down. He's not a game beast, as
I tell ye. But they aint allus killed on the spot. I've
seed niggers take a long saplin' an' make a little split
in it about the middle of the pole, an' stick the end of
a 'possum's long rat-tail through the split an' carry
him home. I've seed two niggers carryin' a pole that
a-way, one at each end, with two or three 'possums
a-hangin' frum it. They take 'em home and fatten
'em. I hate a 'possum, principally fur his tail. Ef it
was curled up short an' had a knot in it, it would be
more like a pig's tail, an' then it would seem as ef the
thing was meant to eat. But the way they have it,
it's like nothing in the whole world but a rat's tail.

"So, as I tell ye, ef thet was a 'possum thet we
treed nex', ther' wasn't no fight, an' some of the niggers got some meat. But after that — I remember it
was about the middle o' the night — we got off again,
this time really arter Haskinses 'coon. I was dead
sure of it. The dogs went diff'rent, too. They was
jist full o' fire an' blood, an'run ahead like as ef they
was mad. They know'd they wasn't on the track of
no common 'coon, this time. As fur all uv us men,
black *an*' white, we jist got up an' got arter them dogs,
an' some o' the little fellers got stuck in a swamp,
down by a branch that runs out o' Haskinses woods
into Widder Thorp's corn-field; but we didn't stop
fur nuthin', an' they never ketched up. We kep' on

down that branch an' through the whole corn-field, an'
then the dogs they took us crossways up a hill, whar
we had to cross two or three gullies, an' I like to broke
my neck down one uv 'em, fur I was in sich a blamed
hurry that I tried to jump across, an' the bank giv' way
on the other side, as I might 'a' know'd it would, an'
down I come, backward. But I landed on two niggers
at the bottom of the gully, an' that kinder broke my
fall, an' I was up an' a-goin' ag'in afore you'd 'a'
know'd it.

"Well, as I tell ye, we jist b'iled up that hill, an'
then we struck inter the widder's woods, which is the
wust woods in the whole world, I reckon, fur runnin'
through arter a pack o' dogs. The whole place was
so growed up with chinkerpin-bushes and dog-wood,
an' every other kind o' underbrush that a hog would
'a' sp'iled his temper goin' through thar in the day-
time; but we jist r'ared an' plunged through them
bushes right on to the tails o' the dogs: an' ef any uv
us had had good clothes on, they'd 'a' been tore off
our backs. But ole clothes won't tear, an' we didn't
care ef they did. The dogs had a hot scent, an' I tell
ye, we was close on to 'em when they got to the critter.
An' what d'ye s'pose the critter was? It was a dog-
arned 'possum in a trap!

"It was a trap sot by ole Uncle Enoch Peters, that
lived on Widder Thorp's farm. He's dead now, but
I remember him fust-rate. He had an' ole mother
over in Cumberland, an' he was the very oldest man
in this country, an' I reckon in the whole world, that
had a livin' mother. Well, that there sneakin' 'pos-

sum had gone snifflin' along through the corn-field, an' up that hill, an' along the gullies, and through that onearthly woods to Uncle Enoch's trap, an' we'd follered him as ef he'd had a store order fur a bar'l o' flour tied to his tail.

"Well, he didn't last long, for the dogs and the niggers, between 'em, tore that trap all to bits; and what become o' the 'possum I don't b'lieve anybody knowed, 'cept it was ole Chink and two or three uv the biggest dogs."

I here asked if 'coons were ever caught in traps.

"Certainly they is," said Martin. "I remember the time that ther' was a good many 'coons caught in traps. That was in the ole Henry Clay 'lection times. The 'coon, he was the Whig beast. He stood for Harry Clay and the hull Whig party. Ther' never was a pole-raisin', or a barbecue, or a speech meetin', or a torch-light percession, in the whole country, that they didn't want a live 'coon to be sot on a pole or some-whar whar the people could look at him an' be encouraged. But it didn't do 'em no good. Ole Harry Clay he went under, an' ye couldn't sell a 'coon for a dime.

"Well, as I tell ye, this was a 'possum in a trap, and we was all pretty mad and pretty tired. We got out on the edge o' the woods as soon as we could, an' thar was a field o' corn. The corn had been planted late and the boys found a lot o' roastin' ears, though they was purty old, but we didn't care for that. We made a fire, an' roasted the corn, an' some o' the men had their ' ticklers ' along, — enough to give us each a taste, — an' we lighted our pipes and sat down to take a rest afore startin' off ag'in arter Haskinses 'coon.''

" But I thought you said,'' I remarked, '' that you knew you were after Haskins' 'coon the last time.''

'' Well, so we did know we was. But sometimes you know things as isn't so. Didn't ye ever find that out? It's so, anyway, jist as I tell ye,'' and then he continued his story :

'' As we was a-settin' aroun' the fire, a-smokin' away, Uncle Pete Williams — he was the feller that had to hang on to the big dog, Chink, as I tell ye — he come an' he says, ' Now, look-a-here, Mahsr Tom, an' de rest ob you all, don't ye bleab we'd better gib up dis yere thing an' go home?' Well, none uv us thought that, an' we told him so ; but he kep' on, an' begun to tell us we'd find ourselves in a heap o' misery, ef we didn't look out, pretty soon. Says he : ' Now, look-a-here, Mahsr Tom, and you all, you all wouldn't a-ketched me out on this yere hunt ef I 'a' knowed ye was a-gwine to hunt 'possums. 'Taint no luck to hunt 'possums : everybody knows dat. De debbil gits after a man as will go a-chasin' 'possums wid dogs when he kin cotch 'em a heap mau comforta-bler in a trap. 'Taint so much diff'rence 'bout 'coons, but the debbil he takes care o' 'possums. An' I spect de debbel know'd 'bout dis yere hunt, fur de oder ebenin' I was a-goin' down to de rock-spring, wid a gourd to git a drink, and dar on de rock, wid his legs a-danglin' down to de water, sat de debbil hisself a-chawin' green terbacker !'—'Green terbacker?' says I. ' Why, Uncle Pete, aint the debbil got no better

sense than that?'— 'Now, look-a-here, Mahsr Martin,'
says he, 'de debbil knows what he's about, an' ef green
terbacker was good fur anybody to chaw he wouldn't
chaw it, an' he says to me, " Uncle Pete, been
a-huntin' any 'possums?" An' says I, " No, Mahsr,
I nebber do dat." An' den he look at me awful, fur I
seed he didn't furgit nothin', an' he was a-sottin' dar,
a-shinen as ef he was polished all over wid shoe-
blackin', an' he says, " Now, look-a-here, Uncle Pete,
don't you eber do it; an' w'at's dat about dis yere
Baptis' church at de Cross-roads, dat was sot afire?"
An' I tole him dat I didn't know nuffin 'bout dat —
not one single word in dis whole world. Den he wink,
an' he says, " Dem bruders in dat church hunt too
many 'possums. Dey is allus a-huntin' 'possums, an'
dat's de way dey lose der church. I sot dat church
afire mesef. D'y' hear dat, Uncle Pete?" An' I was
glad enough to hear it, too ; for der was bruders in dat
church dat said Yeller Joe an' me sot it afire, cos we
wasn't 'lected trustees, but dey can't say dat now, fur
it's all plain as daylight, an' ef dey don't bleab it, I
kin show 'em de berry gourd I tuk down to de rock-
spring when I seed de debbil. An' it don't do to hunt
no more 'possums, fur de debbil'd jist as leab scratch
de end ob his tail ag'in a white man's church as ag'in
a black man's church.'

" By this time we was all ready to start ag'in ; an'
we know'd that all Uncle Pete wanted was to git home
ag'in, fur he was lazy, and was sich an ole rascal that
he was afraid to go back by himself in the dark fur
fear the real debbil'd gobble him up, an' so we didn't

pay no 'tention to him, but jist started off ag'in.
Ther' is niggers as b'lieve the debbil gits after people
that hunt 'possums, but Uncle Pete never b'lieved that
when he was a-goin' to git the 'possum. Ther' wasn't
no chance fur him this night, but he had to come along
all the same, as I tell ye.

"'Twa'n't half an hour arter we started ag'in afore
we found a 'coon, but 'twa'n't Haskinses 'coon. We
was near the crick, when the dogs got arter him, an'
inste'd o' gittin' up a tree, he run up inter the roots uv
a big pine thet had been blown down, and was a-layin'
half in the water. The brush was mighty thick jist
here ; an' some uv us thought it was another 'possum,
an' we kep' back most uv the dogs, fur we didn't want
'em to carry us along that creek-bank arter no 'possum.
But some o' the niggers, with two or three dogs, pushed
through the bushes, and one feller clum up inter the
roots uv the tree, an' out jumped Mr. 'Coon. He
hadn't no chance to git off any other way than to clim'
down some grape-vines that was a-hangin' from the
tree inter the water. So he slips down one o' them,
an' as he was a-hangin' on like a sailor a-goin' down a
rope, I got a look at him through the bushes, an' I see
plain enough by the light-wood torch thet he wa'n't
Haskinses 'coon. He had the commonest kinds o'
bands on his tail.

" Well, that thar 'coon he looked like he was about
the biggest fool uv a coon in this whole world. He
come down to the water, as ef he thought a dog
couldn't swim, an' ef that's what he did think he foun'
out his mistake as soon as he teched the water, fur thar

was a dog ready fur him. An' then they had it lively,
an' the other dogs they jumped in, an' thar was a purty
big splashin' an' plungin' an' bitin' in that thar creek ;
an' I was jist a-goin to push through an' holler fur the
other fellers to come an' see the fun, when that thar
'coon he got off! He jist licked them dogs — the
meanest dogs we had along — an' put fur the other
bank, an' that was the end o' him. 'Coons is a good
deal like folks — it don't pay to call none uv 'em fools
till ye're done seein' what they're up to.

"Well, as I tell ye, we was then nigh the crick ; but
soon as we lef' the widder's woods we struck off from
it, fur none uv us, 'specially the niggers. wanted to go
nigh 'Lijah Parker's. Reckon ye don't know 'Lijah
Parker. Well, he lives 'bout three mile from here on
the crick ; an' he was then, an' is now, jist the laziest
man in the whole world. He had two or three big red
oaks on his place thet he wanted cut down, but was
too durned lazy to do it ; an' he hadn't no money to hire
anybody to do it, nuther, an' he was too stingy to
spend it ef he'd had it. So he know'd ther' was a-goin
to be a 'coon-hunt one night ; an' the evenin' before he
tuk a 'coon his boy'd caught in a 'possum-trap, an'
he put a chain aroun' its body, and pulled it through his
woods to one of his red oak trees. Then he let the
'coon climb up a little ways, an' then he jerked him
down ag'in, and pulled him over to another tree, and so
on, till he'd let him run up three big trees. Then his
boy got a box, an' they put the 'coon in an' carried
him home. Uv course, when the dogs come inter his
woods — an' he know'd they was a-goin to do that —

they got on the scent o' this 'coon; an' when they got to the fust tree, they thought they'd treed him, an' the niggers cut down that red oak in no time. An' then' when ther' wa'n't no 'coon thar, they tracked him to the nex' tree, an' so on till the whole three trees was cut down. We wouldn't 'a' found out nuthin' about this ef 'Lijah's boy hadn't told on the ole man, an' ye kin jist bet all ye're wuth that ther' aint a man in this county that 'u'd cut one o' his trees down ag'in.

"Well, as I tell ye, we kep' clear o' Parker's place, an' we walked about two mile, an' then we found we'd gone clean around till we'd got inter Haskinses woods ag'in. We hadn't gone further inter the woods than ye could pitch a rock afore the dogs got on the track uv a 'coon, an' away we all went arter 'em. Even the little fellers that was stuck in the swamp away back was with us now, fur they got out an' was a-pokin' home through the woods. 'Twa'n't long afore that 'coon was treed; an' when we got up an' looked at the tree, we all felt dead sure it was Haskinses 'coon this time an' no mistake. Fur it was jist the kind o' tree that no 'coon but that 'coon would ever 'a' thought o'climbin'. Mos' 'coons and 'possums shin it up a pretty tall tree, to git as fur away frum the dogs as they kin, an' the tall trees is often purty slim trees an' easy cut down. But this here 'coon o' Haskinses he had more sense than that. He jist skooted up the thickest tree he could find. He didn't care about gittin' up high. He know'd the dogs couldn't climb no tree at all, an' that no man or boy was a-comin' up after him. So he wanted to give 'em the best job

o' choppin he know'd how. Ther' aint no smarter
critter than 'coons in this whole world. Dogs aint no
circumstance to 'em. About four or five year ago, I
was a-livin' with Riley Marsh, over by the Court-house ;
an' his wife she had a tame 'coon, an' this little beast
was a mighty lot smarter than any human bein' in the
house. Sometimes, when he'd come it a little too
heavy with his tricks, they used to chain him up, but
he always got loose and come a humpin' inter the
house with a bit o' the chain to his collar. D'ye know
how a 'coon walks? He never comes straight ahead
like a Christian, but he humps up his back, an' he
twists roun' his tail, an' he sticks out his head, crooked
like, frum under his ha'r, an' he comes inter a room
sideways an' a kind o' cross, as ef he'd a-wanted ter
stay out an' play an' ye'd made him come in the
house ter learn his lessons.

" Well, as I tell ye, this 'coon broke his chain ev'ry
time, an' it was a good thick dog-chain, an' that puzzled Riley ; but one day he saw the little runt goin'
aroun' an' aroun' hoppin' over his chain ev'ry time,
till he got an awful big twist on his chain, an' then it
was easy enough to strain on it till a link opened. But
Riley put a swivel on his chain, an' stopped that fun.
But they'd let him out purty often ; an' one day he
squirmed himself inter the kitchen, an' thar he see the
tea-kittle a-settin' by the fireplace. The lid was off,
an' ole 'cooney thought that was jist the kind uv a
black hole he'd been used to crawlin' inter afore he
got tame. So he crawled in an' curled himself up an'
went to sleep. Arter a while, in comes Aunt Hannah

to git supper; an' she picks up the kittle, an' findin it heavy, thinks it was full o' water, an' puts on the lid an' hung it over the fire. Then she clapped on some light-wood to hurry up things. Purty soon that kittle begun to warm; an' then, all uv a sudden, off pops the lid, an' out shoots Mister 'Coon like a rocket. An' ther' never was, in all this whole world, sich a frightened ole nigger as Aunt Hannah. She thought it was the debbil, sure, an' she giv' a yell that fetched ev'ry man on the place. That ere 'coon had more mischief in him than any live thing ye ever see. He'd pick pockets, hide ev'ry thing he could find, an' steal eggs. He'd find an egg ef the hen 'u'd sneak off an' lay it at the bottom uv the crick. One Sunday, Riley's wife went to all-day preachin' at Hornorsville, an' she put six mockin'-birds she was a-raisin' in one cage; an', fur fear the coon' 'u'd git 'em, she hung the cage frum a hook in the middle uv the ceilin' in the chamber. She had to git upon a chair to do it. Well, she went to preachin', an' that 'coon he got inter the house an' eat up ev'ry one o' them mockin'-birds. Ther' wasn't no tellin' 'xactly how he done it; but we reckoned he got up on the high mantel-piece an' made one big jump from thar to the cage, an' hung on till he put his paw through an' hauled out one bird. Then he dropped an' eat that, an' made anuther jump, till they was all gone. Anyway, he got all the birds, an' that was the last meal he ever eat.

" Well, as I tell ye, that 'coon he got inter the thickest tree in the whole woods; an' thar he sat a-peepin' at us from a crotch that wasn't twenty feet frum the

ground. Young Charley Ferris he took a burnin'
chunk that one o' the boys had fetched along frum
the fire, an' throw'd it up at him, 'at we could all
see him plain. He was Haskinses 'coon, sure. There
wasn't a stripe on his tail. Arter that, the niggers
jist made them axes swing, I tell ye. They had a big
job afore 'em; but they took turns at it, an' didn't
waste no time. An' the rest uv us we got the dogs
ready. We wasn't a-goin' to let this 'coon off this
here time. No, sir! Ther' was too many dogs, as I
tell ye, an' we had four or five uv the clumsiest uv 'em
tuk a little way off, with boys to hole 'em; an' the
other dogs an' the hounds, 'specially old Chink, was
held ready to tackle the 'coon when the time come.
An' we had to be mighty sharp about this, too, fur we
all saw that that thar 'coon was a-goin' to put the minute the tree come down. He wasn't goin' to git in a
hole an' be cut out. Ther' didn't 'pear to be any hole,
an' he didn't want none. All he wanted was a good
thick tree an' a crotch to set in an' think. That was
what he was a-doin'. He was cunjerin' up some trick
or other. We all know'd that, but we jist made up
our minds to be ready fur him; an' though, as he was
Haskinses 'coon, the odds was ag'in us, we was dead
sure we'd git him this time.

"I thought that thar tree never *was* a comin' down;
but purty soon it began to crack and lean, and then
down she come. Ev'ry dog, man, an' boy, made a
rush fur that crotch, but ther' was no coon thar. As
the tree come down he seed how the land lay; and
quicker'n any light'in' in this whole world he jist

streaked the other way to the root o' the tree, giv' one
hop over the stump, an' was off. I seed him do it,
an' the dogs see him, but they wasn't quick enough,
and couldn't stop 'emselves — they was goin' so hard
fur the crotch.

" Ye never did see in all yer days sech a mad crowd
as that thar crowd around that tree, but they didn't
stop none to sw'ar. The dogs was arter the 'coon,
an' arter him we went too. He put fur the edge of the
woods, which looked queer, fur a coon never will go
out into the open if he kin help it; but the dogs
was so hot arter him that he couldn't run fur, and he
was treed ag'in in less than five minutes. This time
he was in a tall hick'ry-tree, right on the edge o' the
woods; and it wa'n't a very thick tree, nuther, so the
niggers they jist tuk ther' axes, but afore they could
make a single crack, ole Haskins he runs at 'em an'
pushes 'em away.

" ' Don't ye touch that thar tree ! ' he hollers. ' That
hick'ry marks my line ! ' An' sure enough, that was
the tree with the surveyors' cuts on it, that marked
the place where the line took a corner that run atween
Haskinses farm and Widder Thorp's. He know'd the
tree the minute he seed it, an' so did I, fur I carried
the chain for the surveyors when they laid off the line ;
an' we could all see the cut they'd blazed on it, fur it
was fresh yit, an' it was gittin' to be daylight now, an'
we could see things plain.

" Well, as I tell ye, ev'ry man uv us jist r'ared and
snorted, an' the dogs an' boys was madder'n the rest
uv us, but ole Haskins he didn't give in. He jist

walked aroun' that tree an' wouldn't let a nigger touch
it. He said he wanted to kill the 'coon jist as much
as anybody, but he wasn't a-goin to have his line
sp'iled, arter the money he'd spent, fur all the 'coons
in this whole world.

"Now did ye ever hear of sich a cute trick as that?
That thar 'coon he must 'a' knowed that was Haskinses
line-tree, an' I spect he'd 'a' made fur it fust, ef he'd
a-knowed ole Haskins was along. But he didn't know
it, till he was a-settin' in the crotch uv the big tree
and could look aroun' an' see who was thar. It
wouldn't 'a' been no use fur him to go for that hick'ry
if Haskins hadn't 'a' bin thar, for he know'd well
enough it 'u'd 'a' come down sure."

I smiled at this statement, but Martin shook his
head.

"'Twon't do," he said, "to undervally the sense of
no 'coon. How're ye goin to tell what he knows? Well,
as I tell ye, we was jist gittin' madder an' madder
when a nigger named Wash Webster, he run out in the
field, — it was purty light now, as I tell ye — an' he
hollers, 'O, Mahsr Tom! Mahsr Tom! Dat ar 'coon
he aint you 'coon! He got stripes to he tail!'

"We all made a rush out inter the field, to try to
git a look; an' sure enough we could see the little
beast a-settin' up in a crotch over on that side, an' I
do b'lieve he knowed what we was all a-lookin' up fur,
fur he jist kind a lowered his tail out o' the crotch so's
we could see it, an' thar it was, striped, jist like any
cther coon's tail."

"And you were so positively sure this time, that it

was Haskins' 'coon,'' I said. "Why, you saw, when the man threw the blazing chunk into the big tree, that it had no bands on its tail.''

"That's so,'' said Martin ; " but ther' aint no man that kin see 'xactly straight uv a dark mornin', with no light but a flyin' chunk, and 'specially when he wants to see somethin' that isn't thar. An' as to bein' certain about that 'coon, I jist tell ye that ther's nothin' a man's more like to be mistook about, than a thing he knows fur dead sure.

" Well, as I tell ye, when we seed that that thar 'coon wa'n't Haskinses 'coon, arter all, an' that we couldn't git him out er that tree as long as the ole man was thar, we jist give up and put across the field for Haskinses house, whar we was a-goin' to git breakfus'. Some of the boys and the dogs staid aroun' the tree, but ole Haskins he ordered 'em off an' wouldn't let nobody stay thar, though they had a mighty stretchin' time gittin' the dogs away.''

" It seems to me,'' said I, " that there wasn't much profit in that hunt.''

" Well,'' said Martin, putting his pipe in his pocket, and feeling under his chair for his string of fish, which must have been pretty dry and stiff by this time, " the fun in a 'coon-hunt aint so much in gittin' the 'coon, as goin' arter him — which is purty much the same in a good many other things, as I tell ye.''

And he took up his fish and departed.

HIS WIFE'S DECEASED SISTER.

IT is now five years since an event occurred which
so colored my life, or rather so changed some of
its original colors, that I have thought it well to write
an account of it. deeming that its lessons may be of
advantage to persons whose situations in life are similar to my own.

When I was quite a young man I adopted literature as a profession; and having passed through the
necessary preparatory grades, I found myself, after a
good many years of hard, and often unremunerative
work, in possession of what might be called a fair
literary practice. My articles, grave, gay, practical,
or fanciful, had come to be considered with a favor
by the editors of the various periodicals for which I
wrote, on which I found in time I could rely with a
very comfortable certainty. My productions created
no enthusiasm in the reading public; they gave me no
great reputation or very valuable pecuniary return;
but they were always accepted, and my receipts from
them, at the time to which I have referred, were as
regular and reliable as a salary, and quite sufficient
to give me more than a comfortable support.

It was at this time I married.   I had been engaged
for more than a year, but had not been willing to assume the support of a wife until I felt that my pecuniary position was so assured that I could do so with
full satisfaction to my own conscience.   There was
now no doubt in regard to this position, either in my
mind or in that of my wife.   I worked with great
steadiness and regularity; I knew exactly where to
place the productions of my pen, and could calculate,
with a fair degree of accuracy, the sums I should
receive for them.   We were by no means rich ; but
we had enough, and were thoroughly satisfied and
content.

Those of my readers who are married will have no
difficulty in remembering the peculiar ecstasy of the
first weeks of their wedded life.   It is then that the
flowers of this world bloom brightest ; that its sun is
the most genial ; that its clouds are the scarcest ; that
its fruit is the most delicious ; that the air is the most
balmy ; that its cigars are of the highest flavor ; that
the warmth and radiance of early matrimonial felicity
so rarefies the intellectual atmosphere, that the soul
mounts higher, and enjoys a wider prospect, than ever
before.

These experiences were mine.   The plain claret of
my mind was changed to sparkling champagne, and
at the very height of its effervescence I wrote a story.
The happy thought that then struck me for a tale was
of a very peculiar character ; and it interested me so
much that I went to work at it with great delight and
enthusiasm, and finished it in a comparatively short

time. The title of the story was "His Wife's Deceased Sister;" and when I read it to Hypatia she was delighted with it, and at times was so affected by its pathos that her uncontrollable emotion caused a sympathetic dimness in my eyes, which prevented my seeing the words I had written. When the reading was ended, and my wife had dried her eyes, she turned to me and said, "This story will make your fortune. There has been nothing so pathetic since Lamartine's ' History of a Servant-Girl.' "

As soon as possible the next day I sent my story to the editor of the periodical for which I wrote most frequently, and in which my best productions generally appeared. In a few days I had a letter from the editor, in which he praised my story as he had never before praised any thing from my pen. It had interested and charmed, he said, not only himself, but all his associates in the office. Even old Gibson, who never cared to read any thing until it was in proof, and who never praised any thing which had not a joke in it, was induced by the example of the others to read this manuscript, and shed, as he asserted, the first tears that had come from his eyes since his final paternal castigation some forty years before. The story would appear, the editor assured me, as soon as he could possibly find room for it.

If any thing could make our skies more genial, our flowers brighter, and the flavor of our fruit and cigars more delicious, it was a letter like this. And when, in a very short time, the story was published, we found that the reading public was inclined to receive it with as much sympathetic interest and favor as had been shown to it by the editors. My personal friends soon began to express enthusiastic opinions upon it. It was highly praised in many of the leading newspapers; and, altogether, it was a great literary success. I am not inclined to be vain of my writings, and, in general, my wife tells me, think too little of them; but I did feel a good deal of pride and satisfaction in the success of " His Wife's Deceased Sister." If it did not make my fortune, as my wife asserted that it would, it certainly would help me very much in my literary career.

In less than a month from the writing of this story, something very unusual and unexpected happened to me. A manuscript was returned by the editor of the periodical in which " His Wife's Deceased Sister " had appeared. " It is a good story," he wrote, " but not equal to what you have just done. You have made a great hit; and it would not do to interfere with the reputation you have gained, by publishing any thing inferior to ' His Wife's Deceased Sister,' which has had such a deserved success."

I was so unaccustomed to having my work thrown back on my hands, that I think I must have turned a little pale when I read the letter. I said nothing of the matter to my wife, for it would be foolish to drop such grains of sand as this into the smoothly oiled machinery of our domestic felicity; but I immediately sent the story to another editor. I am not able to express the astonishment I felt, when, in the course of a week, it was sent back to me. The tone of the note accompanying it indicated a somewhat injured feeling on the part of the editor. " I am reluctant," he said. " to decline a manuscript from you ; but you know very well that if you sent me any thing like ' His Wife's Deceased Sister ' it would be most promptly accepted."

I now felt obliged to speak of the affair to my wife, who was quite as much surprised, though, perhaps, not quite as much shocked, as I had been.

" Let us read the story again," she said, " and see what is the matter with it." When we had finished its perusal, Hypatia remarked : " It is quite as good as many of the stories you have had printed, and I think it very interesting ; although, of course, it is not equal to ' His Wife's Deceased Sister.' "

" Of course not," said I, " that was an inspiration that I cannot expect every day. But there must be something wrong about this last story which we do not perceive. Perhaps my recent success may have made me a little careless in writing it."

" I don't believe that," said Hypatia.

" At any rate," I continued, " I will lay it aside, and will go to work on a new one."

In due course of time I had another manuscript finished, and I sent it to my favorite periodical. It was retained some weeks, and then came back to me. " It will never do," the editor wrote, quite warmly, " for you to go backward. The demand for the number containing ' His Wife's Deceased Sister ' still continues, and we do not intend to let you disappoint that great body of readers who would be so eager to see another number containing one of your stories."

I sent this manuscript to four other periodicals, and from each of them was it returned with remarks to the effect, that, although it was not a bad story in itself, it was not what they would expect from the author of "His Wife's Deceased Sister."

The editor of a Western magazine wrote to me for a story to be published in a special number which he would issue for the holidays. I wrote him one of the character and length he asked for, and sent it to him. By return mail it came back to me. "I had hoped." the editor wrote, "when I asked for a story from your pen, to receive something like 'His Wife's Deceased Sister,' and I must own that I am very much disappointed."

I was so filled with anger when I read this note, that I openly objurgated "His Wife's Deceased Sister." "You must excuse me," I said to my astonished wife, "for expressing myself thus in your presence; but that confounded story will be the ruin of me yet. Until it is forgotten nobody will ever take any thing I write."

"And you cannot expect it ever to be forgotten," said Hypatia, with tears in her eyes.

It is needless for me to detail my literary efforts in the course of the next few months. The ideas of the editors with whom my principal business had been done, in regard to my literary ability, had been so raised by my unfortunate story of "His Wife's Deceased Sister," that I found it was of no use to send them any thing of lesser merit. And as to the other journals which I tried, they evidently considered it an

insult for me to send them matter inferior to that by
which my reputation had lately risen. The fact was
that my successful story had ruined me. My income
was at end, and want actually stared me in the face;
and I must admit that I did not like the expression
of its countenance. It was of no use for me to try
to write another story like " His Wife's Deceased
Sister." I could not get married every time I began
a new manuscript, and it was the exaltation of mind
caused by my wedded felicity which produced that
story.

"It's perfectly dreadful!" said my wife. "If I
had had a sister, and she had died, I would have
thought it was my fault."

"It could not be your fault," I answered, "and I
do not think it was mine. I had no intention of
deceiving anybody into the belief that I could do
that sort of thing every time, and it ought not to be
expected of me. Suppose Raphael's patrons had tried
to keep him screwed up to the pitch of the Sistine
Madonna, and had refused to buy any thing which
was not as good as that. In that case I think he
would have occupied a much earlier and narrower
grave than that on which Mr. Morris Moore hangs
his funeral decorations."

"But, my dear," said Hypatia, who was posted on
such subjects, "the Sistine Madonna was one of his
latest paintings."

"Very true," said I; "but if he had married, as I
did, he would have painted it earlier."

I was walking homeward one afternoon about this

time, when I met Barbel, — a man I had known well
in my early literary career. He was now about fifty
years of age, but looked older. His hair and beard
were quite gray; and his clothes, which were of the
same general hue, gave me the idea that they, like his
hair, had originally been black. Age is very hard on
a man's external appointments. Barbel had an air
of having been to let for a long time, and quite out of
repair. But there was a kindly gleam in his eye, and
he welcomed me cordially.

"Why, what is the matter, old fellow?" said he.
"I never saw you look so woe-begone."

I had no reason to conceal any thing from Barbel.
In my younger days he had been of great use to me,
and he had a right to know the state of my affairs. I
laid the whole case plainly before him.

"Look here," he said, when I had finished, "come
with me to my room: I have something I would like
to say to you there."

I followed Barbel to his room. It was at the top
of a very dirty and well-worn house, which stood in a
narrow and lumpy street, into which few vehicles ever
penetrated, except the ash and garbage carts, and the
rickety wagons of the venders of stale vegetables.

"This is not exactly a fashionable promenade," said
Barbel, as we approached the house; "but in some
respects it reminds me of the streets in Italian towns,
where the palaces lean over towards each other in such
a friendly way."

Barbel's room was, to my mind, rather more doleful
than the street. It was dark, it was dusty, and cob-

webs hung from every corner. The few chairs upon
the floor and the books upon a greasy table seemed to
be afflicted with some dorsal epidemic, for their backs
were either gone or broken. A little bedstead in the
corner was covered with a spread made of "New-
York Heralds," with their edges pasted together.

"There is nothing better," said Barbel, noticing my
glance towards this novel counterpane, "for a bed-
covering than newspapers : they keep you as warm as
a blanket, and are much lighter. I used to use "Tri-
bunes," but they rattled too much."

The only part of the room which was well lighted
was at one end near the solitary window. Here, upon
a table with a spliced leg, stood a little grindstone.

"At the other end of the room," said Barbel, "is
my cook-stove, which you can't see unless I light the
candle in the bottle which stands by it; but if you
don't care particularly to examine it, I won't go to the
expense of lighting up. You might pick up a good
many odd pieces of bric-à-brac around here, if you
chose to strike a match and investigate ; but I would
not advise you to do so. It would pay better to throw
the things out of the window than to carry them down
stairs. The particular piece of in-door decoration to
which I wish to call your attention is this." And he
led me to a little wooden frame which hung against
the wall near the window. Behind a dusty piece of
glass it held what appeared to be a leaf from a small
magazine or journal. "There," said he, "you see
a page from ' The Grasshopper,' a humorous paper
which flourished in this city some half-dozen years

ago. I used to write regularly for that paper, as you
may remember.''

'' Oh, yes, indeed ! '' I exclaimed. '' And I shall
never forget your ' Conundrum of the Anvil ' which
appeared in it. How often have I laughed at that most
wonderful conceit, and how often have I put it to my
friends ! ''

Barbel gazed at me silently for a moment, and then
he pointed to the frame. '' That printed page,'' he
said solemnly, '' contains the ' Conundrum of the Anvil.' I hang it there, so that I can see it while I work.
That conundrum ruined me. It was the last thing I
wrote for ' The Grasshopper.' How I ever came to
imagine it, I cannot tell. It is one of those things
which occur to a man but once in a lifetime. After
the wild shout of delight with which the public greeted
that conundrum, my subsequent efforts met with hoots
of derision. ' The Grasshopper ' turned its hind-legs
upon me. I sank from bad to worse, — much worse,
until at last I found myself reduced to my present
occupation, which is that of grinding points to pins.
By this I procure my bread, coffee, and tobacco, and
sometimes potatoes and meat. One day while I was
hard at work, an organ-grinder came into the street
below. He played the serenade from Trovatore ; and
the familiar notes brought back visions of old days
and old delights, when the successful writer wore good
clothes and sat at operas, when he looked into sweet
eyes and talked of Italian airs, when his future appeared all a succession of bright scenery and joyous
acts, without any provision for a drop-curtain. And as

my ear listened, and my mind wandered in this happy
retrospect, my every faculty seemed exalted, and, without any thought upon the matter, I ground points upon
my pins so fine, so regular, and smooth, that they would
have pierced with ease the leather of a boot, or slipped
among, without abrasion, the finest threads of rare old
lace. When the organ stopped, and I fell back into
my real world of cobwebs and mustiness, I gazed upon
the pins I had just ground, and, without a moment's
hesitation, I threw them into the street, and reported
the lot as spoiled. This cost me a little money, but it
saved me my livelihood."

After a few moments of silence, Barbel resumed, —
"I have no more to say to you, my young friend.
All I want you to do is to look upon that framed
conundrum, then upon this grindstone, and then to
go home and reflect. As for me, I have a gross of
pins to grind before the sun goes down."

I cannot say that my depression of mind was at all
relieved by what I had seen and heard. I had lost
sight of Barbel for some years, and I had supposed
him still floating on the sun-sparkling stream of prosperity where I had last seen him. It was a great
shock to me to find him in such a condition of pov-
erty and squalor, and to see a man who had originated
the "Conundrum of the Anvil" reduced to the soul-
depressing occupation of grinding pin-points. As I
walked and thought, the dreadful picture of a totally
eclipsed future arose before my mind. The moral of
Barbel sank deep into my heart.

When I reached home I told my wife the story of

my friend Barbel. She listened with a sad and eager interest.

"I am afraid," she said, "if our fortunes do not quickly mend, that we shall have to buy two little grindstones. You know I could help you at that sort of thing."

For a long time we sat together and talked, and devised many plans for the future. I did not think it necessary yet for me to look out for a pin-contract; but I must find some way of making money, or we should starve to death. Of course, the first thing that suggested itself was the possibility of finding some other business; but, apart from the difficulty of immediately obtaining remunerative work in occupations to which I had not been trained, I felt a great and natural reluctance to give up a profession for which I had carefully prepared myself, and which I had adopted as my life-work. It would be very hard for me to lay down my pen forever, and to close the top of my inkstand upon all the bright and happy fancies which I had seen mirrored in its tranquil pool. We talked and pondered the rest of that day and a good deal of the night, but we came to no conclusion as to what it would be best for us to do.

The next day I determined to go and call upon the editor of the journal for which, in happier days, before the blight of "His Wife's Deceased Sister" rested upon me, I used most frequently to write, and, having frankly explained my condition to him, to ask his advice. The editor was a good man, and had always been my friend. He listened with great attention to what I told him, and evidently sympathized with me in my trouble.

"As we have written to you," he said, "the only reason why we did not accept the manuscripts you sent us was, that they would have disappointed the high hopes that the public had formed in regard to you. We have had letter after letter asking when we were going to publish another story like 'His Wife's Deceased Sister.' We felt, and we still feel, that it would be wrong to allow you to destroy the fair fabric which yourself has raised. But," he added, with a kind smile, "I see very plainly that your well-deserved reputation will be of little advantage to you if you should starve at the moment that its genial beams are, so to speak, lighting you up."

"Its beams are not genial," I answered. "They have scorched and withered me."

"How would you like," said the editor, after a short reflection, "to allow us to publish the stories you have recently written under some other name than your own? That would satisfy us and the public, would put money in your pocket, and would not interfere with your reputation."

Joyfully I seized that noble fellow by the hand, and instantly accepted his proposition. "Of course," said I "a reputation is a very good thing; but no reputation can take the place of food, clothes, and a house to live in; and I gladly agree to sink my over-illumined name into oblivion, and to appear before the public as a new and unknown writer."

"I hope that need not be for long," he said, "for

I feel sure that you will yet write stories as good as 'His Wife's Deceased Sister.'"

All the manuscripts I had on hand I now sent to my good friend the editor, and in due and proper order they appeared in his journal under the name of John Darmstadt, which I had selected as a substitute for my own, permanently disabled. I made a similar arrangement with other editors, and John Darmstadt received the credit of every thing that proceeded from my pen. Our circumstances now became very comfortable, and occasionally we even allowed ourselves to indulge in little dreams of prosperity.

Time passed on very pleasantly; one year, another, and then a little son was born to us. It is often difficult, I believe, for thoughtful persons to decide whether the beginning of their conjugal career, or the earliest weeks in the life of their first-born, be the happiest and proudest period of their existence. For myself I can only say that the same exaltation of mind, the same rarefication of idea and invention, which succeeded upon my wedding-day came upon me now. As then, my ecstatic emotions crystallized themselves into a motive for a story, and without delay I set myself to work upon it. My boy was about six weeks old when the manuscript was finished; and one evening, as we sat before a comfortable fire in our sitting-room, with the curtains drawn, and the soft lamp lighted, and the baby sleeping soundly in the adjoining chamber, I read the story to my wife.

When I had finished, my wife arose, and threw herself into my arms. "I was never so proud of you," she said, her glad eyes sparkling, "as I am at this moment. That is a wonderful story! It is, indeed I am sure it is, just as good as ' His Wife's Deceased Sister.'"

As she spoke these words, a sudden and chilling sensation crept over us both. All her warmth and fervor, and the proud and happy glow engendered within me by this praise and appreciation from one I loved, vanished in an instant. We stepped apart, and gazed upon each other with pallid faces. In the same moment the terrible truth had flashed upon us both.

This story *was* as good as " His Wife's Deceased Sister " !

We stood silent. The exceptional lot of Barbel's super-pointed pins seemed to pierce our very souls. A dreadful vision rose before me of an impending fall and crash, in which our domestic happiness should vanish, and our prospects for our boy be wrecked, just as we had begun to build them up.

My wife approached me, and took my hand in hers, which was as cold as ice. " Be strong and firm," she said. " A great danger threatens us, but you must brace yourself against it. Be strong and firm."

I pressed her hand, and we said no more that night.

The next day I took the manuscript I had just written, and carefully enfolded it in stout wrapping-paper. Then I went to a neighboring grocery store, and bought a small, strong, tin box, originally intended for biscuit, with a cover that fitted tightly. In this I placed my manuscript; and then I took the box to a tinsmith, and had the top fastened on with hard solder. When

I went home I ascended into the garret, and brought down to my study a ship's cash-box, which had once belonged to one of my family who was a sea-captain. This box was very heavy, and firmly bound with iron, and was secured by two massive locks. Calling my wife, I told her of the contents of the tin case, which I then placed in the box, and, having shut down the heavy lid, I doubly locked it.

"This key," said I, putting it in my pocket, "I shall throw into the river when I go out this afternoon."

My wife watched me eagerly, with a pallid and firm, set countenance, but upon which I could see the faint glimmer of returning happiness.

"Wouldn't it be well," she said, "to secure it still further by sealing-wax and pieces of tape?"

"No," said I. "I do not believe that any one will attempt to tamper with our prosperity. And now, my dear," I continued in an impressive voice, "no one but you, and, in the course of time, our son, shall know that this manuscript exists. When I am dead, those who survive me may, if they see fit, cause this box to be split open, and the story published. The reputation it may give my name cannot harm me then."

OUR STORY.

I.

I BECAME acquainted with Miss Bessie Vancouver at a reception given by an eminent literary gentleman in New York. The circumstances were a little peculiar. Miss Vancouver and I had each written and recently published a book ; and we were introduced to each other as young authors whose works had made us known to the public, and who, consequently, should know each other. The peculiarity of the situation lay in the fact that I had not read Miss Vancouver's book, nor had she read mine. Consequently, although each felt bound to speak of the work of the other, neither of us could do it except in the most general and cautious way. I was quite sure that her book was a novel, but that was all that I knew about it, except that I had heard it well spoken of ; but she supposed my book was of a scientific character, whereas, in reality, it also was a novel, although its title did not indicate the fact. There was therefore an air of restraint and stiffness about our first interview which it might not have had if we had frankly acknowledged our shortcomings.   But, as the general conversation led her to believe that she was the only person in the room who had not read my book, and me to believe that I was the only one who had not read hers, we were naturally loath to confess the truth to each other.

I next met Miss Vancouver in Paris, at the house of a lady whose parlors are the frequent rendezvous of Americans, especially those given to art or literature. This time we met on different ground.   I had read her book and she mine ; and as soon as we had shaken hands we began to talk of each other's work, not as if it had been the beginning of a new conversation, but rather as the continuation of one broken off.   Each liked the book of the other extremely, and we were free to say so.

"But I am not satisfied with my novel," said Miss Vancouver.   " There is too much oneness about it ; by which I mean that it is not diversified enough.   It is all, or nearly all, about two people, who, of course, have but one object in life ; and it seems to me now that their story might have been finished a great deal sooner, though, of course, in that case it would not have been long enough to make a book."

To this I politely answered that I did not agree with her, for the story was interesting to the very end ; but, of course, if she had put more characters into it, and they had been as good in their way as those she already had, the book would have been that much the better. "As for me," I continued, "my trouble is entirely the other way.   I have no oneness whatever.   My tendency is much more to fifteen or twenty-ness.   I

carry a story a little way in one direction, and then
I stop and go off in another. It is sometimes difficult
to make it understood why a character should have been
brought into the story at all; and I have had a good
deal of trouble in making some of them do something
toward the end to show that they are connected with
the general plot.''

She said she had noticed that there was a wideness
of scope in my book; but what she would have said
further I do not know, for our hostess now came down
upon us and carried off Miss Vancouver to introduce
her to an old lady who had successfully steered about
fifty barques across that sea on which Miss Vancouver
had just set out.

Our next meeting was in a town on the Mediterranean, in the south of France. I had secured board at
a large *pension* there, and was delighted to find that
Miss Bessie Vancouver and her mother were already
inmates of the house. As soon as I had the opportunity, I broached to her an idea which had frequently
possessed my mind since our conversation in Paris. I
proposed that we should write a story together, something like Erckmann-Chatrian, or Mark Twain and Mr.
Warner in "The Gilded Age." Since she had too
much unity of purpose and travelled in too narrow a
path, and I branched off too much, and had too great
a tendency to variety, our styles, if properly blended,
would possess all the qualities needed in a good story;
and there was no reason why we should not, writing
thus together, achieve a success greater, perhaps, than
either of us could expect writing alone. I had thought

so much on this subject that I was able to say a great deal, and to say it pretty well, too, so far as I could judge. Miss Vancouver listened with great attention, and the more I said, the more the idea pleased her. She said she would take the afternoon to consider the matter; and in the evening she told me in the parlor that she had made up her mind, if I still thought well of the plan, to assist me in writing a story, — this being the polite way in which she chose to put it, — but that she thought it would be better for us to begin with a short story, and not with a book, for in this way we could sooner see how we would be likely to succeed. Of course I agreed to this proposition, and we arranged that we should meet the next morning in the garden and lay out a plan for our story.

The garden attached to the house in which we lived was a very quaint and pleasant one. It had been made a hundred years ago or more by an Italian nobleman, whose mansion, now greatly altered, had become our present *pension*. The garden was laid out in a series of terraces on the side of a hill, and abounded in walks shaded by orange and lemon trees, arbors, and vine-covered trellises; fountains, half concealed by overhanging ivy; and suddenly discovered stair-ways, wide and shadowy, leading up into regions of greater quaintness and seclusion. Flowers were here, and palm-trees, and great cactus-bushes, with their red fruit half hollowed out by the nibbling birds. From the upper terraces we could see the blue Mediterranean spreading far away on one side, while the snow-covered tops of the Maritime Alps stood bright against the sky. The garden was little frequented, and altogether it was a good place in which to plan a story.

We consulted together for several days before we actually began to work. At first, we sat in an arbor on one of the lower terraces, where there were a little iron table and some chairs ; but now and then a person would come there for a morning stroll, and so we moved up higher to a seat under a palm-tree, and the next day to another terrace, where there was a secluded corner overshadowed by huge cacti. But the place which suited us best of all was the top of an old tower at one end of the garden. This tower had been built many, many hundred years before the garden was thought of, and its broad, flat roof was level with one of the higher terraces. Here we could work and consult in quiet, with little fear of being disturbed.

Not finding it easy to plan out the whole story at once, we determined to begin by preparing backgrounds. We concluded that as this was to be a short story, it would be sufficient to have descriptions of two natural scenes in which the two principal incidents should occur ; and as we wished to do all our work from natural models, we thought it best to describe the scene which lay around us, than which nothing could be more beautiful or more suitable. One scene was to be on the sea-shore, with a mellow light upon the rippling waves, and the sails of fishing-vessels in the distance. This Miss Vancouver was to do, while I was to take a scene among the hills and mountains at the back of the town. I walked over there one afternoon when Miss Vancouver had gone out with her mother. I got on a high point, and worked up a very satisfactory description of the frowning mountains behind me, the old monasteries on the hills, and the town stretching out below, with a little river rushing along between two rows of picturesque washerwomen to the sea.

We read our backgrounds to each other, and were both very well satisfied. Our styles were as different as the scenes we described. Hers was clear and smooth, and mine forcible and somewhat abrupt, and thus the strong points of each scene were better brought out; but, in order that our styles might be unified, so to speak, by being judiciously blended, I suggested some strong and effective points to be introduced into her description, while she toned down some of my phrases, and added a word here and there which gave a color and beauty to the description which it had not possessed before.

Our backgrounds being thus satisfactory, — and it took a good deal of consultation to make them so, — our next work was to provide characters for the story. These were to be drawn from life, for it would be perfectly ridiculous to create imaginary characters when there were so many original and interesting personages around us. We soon agreed upon an individual who would serve as a model for our hero; I forget whether it was I or Miss Vancouver who first suggested him. He was a young man, but not so very young either, who lived in the house with us, and about whom there was a mystery. Nobody knew exactly who he was, or where he came from, or why he was here. It was evident he did not come for society, for he kept very much to himself ; and the attractions of the town could not have brought him here, for he seemed to care very little about them. We seldom saw him except at the table and occasionally in the garden. When we met him in the latter place, he always seemed anxious to avoid observation ; and as we did not wish to hurt his feelings by letting him suppose that he was an object of curiosity to us, we endeavored, as far as possible, to make it apparent that we were not looking at him or thinking of him. But still, whenever we had a good chance, we studied him. Of course, we could not make out his mystery, but that was not necessary. nor did we, indeed, think it would be proper. We could draw him as we saw him, and then make the mystery what we pleased ; its character depending a good deal upon the plot we devised.

Miss Vancouver undertook to draw the hero, and she went to work upon him immediately. In personal appearance, she altered the model a good deal. She darkened his hair, and took off his whiskers, leaving him only a mustache. She thought, too, that he ought to be a little taller, and asked me my height, which is five feet nine. She considered that a very good height, and brought the hero up to it. She also made him some years younger, but endeavored, as far as seemed suitable to the story, to draw him exactly as he was.

I was to do the heroine, but found it very hard to choose a model. As I said before, we determined to draw all our characters from life, but I could think of no one, in the somewhat extensive company by which we were surrounded, who would answer my purpose. Nor could I fix my mind upon any person in other parts of the world, whom I knew or had known, who resembled the idea I had formed of our heroine. After thinking this matter over a good deal, I told Miss Vancouver that I believed the best thing I could do would be to take her for my model. I was with her a good deal, and thus could study out and work up certain points as I wrote, which would be a great advantage. She objected to this, because, as she said, the author of a story should not be drawn as its heroine. But I asserted that this would not be the case. She would merely suggest the heroine to me, and I would so do my work that the heroine would not suggest her to anybody else. This, I thought, was the way in which a model ought to be used. After we had talked the subject over a good deal, she agreed to my plan, and I went to work with much satisfaction. I gave no definite description of the lady, but endeavored to indicate the impression which her person and character produced upon me. As such impressions are seldom the same in any two cases, there was no danger that my description could be referred back to her.

When I read to her the sketch I had written, she objected to parts of it as not being correct; but as I asserted that it was not intended as an exact copy of the model, she could not say it was not a true picture; and so, with some slight modifications, we let it stand. I thought myself that it was a very good piece of work. To me it seemed very life-like and piquant, and I believed that other people would think it so.

We were now ready for the incidents and the plot, but at this point we were somewhat interrupted by Mrs. Vancouver. She came to me one morning, when I was waiting to go with her daughter to our study in the garden, and told me that she was very sorry to notice that Miss Vancouver and I had attracted attention to ourselves by being so much together ; and, while she understood the nature of the literary labor on which we were engaged, she did not wish her daughter to become the object of general attention and remark in a foreign *pension.* I was very angry when I heard that people had been directing upon us their impertinent curiosity, and I discoursed warmly upon the subject.

" Where is the good," I said, " of a person or persons devoting himself or themselves, with enthusiasm and earnestness, to his or their life-work, if he or they are to be interfered with by the impertinent babble of the multitude? "

Mrs. Vancouver was not prepared to give an exact answer to this question, but she considered the babble of the multitude a very serious thing. She had been talking to her daughter on the subject, and thought it right to speak to me.

That morning we worked separately in our rooms, but we accomplished little or nothing. It was, of course, impossible to do any thing of importance in a work of this kind without consultation and co-operation. The next day, however, I devised a plan which would enable us, I thought, to pursue our labors without attracting attention ; and Mrs. Vancouver, who was a kind-hearted woman, and took a great interest in her daughter's literary career, told me if I could successfully carry out any thing of the kind, I might do so. She did not inquire into particulars, nor did I explain them to Miss Bessie; but I told the latter that we would not go out together into the garden, but I would go first, and she should join me about ten minutes afterward on the tower; but she was not to come if she saw any one about.

Near the top of the hill, above the garden, once stood an ancient mansion, of which nothing now remained but the remnants of some massive masonry. A court-yard, however, of this old edifice was still surrounded by a high wall, which formed the upper boundary of our garden. From a point near the tower a flight of twisting stone steps, flanked by blank walls, which turned themselves in various directions to suit the angles of the stair-way, led to a green door in this wall. Through this door Miss Vancouver and myself, and doubtless many other persons, had often wished to pass; but it was locked, and, on inquiry, we found that there was no key to be had. The day previous, however, when wandering by myself, I had examined this door, and found that it was fastened merely by a snap-lock which had no handle, but was opened by a key. I had a knife with a long, strong blade, and pushing this into the hasp, I easily forced back the bolt. I then opened the door and walked into the old court-yard.

When Miss Vancouver appeared on the tower, I was standing at the top of the stone steps just mentioned,

with the green door slightly ajar. Calling to her in a
low tone, she ran up the steps, and, to her amazement,
I ushered her into the court-yard and closed the door
behind us.

"There," I exultingly exclaimed, "is our study,
where we can write our story without interruption.
We will come and go away separately; the people of
the *pension* will not know that we are here or have
been here, and there will be no occasion for that impertinent attention to which your mother so properly
objects."

Miss Vancouver was delighted, and we walked about
and surveyed the court-yard with much satisfaction.
I had already selected the spot for our work. It was
in the shade of an olive-tree, the only tree in the enclosure, beneath which there was a rude seat. I spread a
rug upon the grass, and Miss Bessie sat upon the seat,
and put her feet upon the rug, leaving room for me to
sit thereon. We now took out our little blank-books
and our stylograph pens and were ready for work. I
explained that I had done nothing the day before, and
Miss Vancouver said that had also been the case with
her. She had not wished to do any thing important
without consultation; but supposing that, of course,
the hero was to fall in love with the heroine, she
thought she might as well make him begin, but she
found she could not do it as she wished. She wanted
him to indicate to the lady that he was in love with her
without exactly saying so. Could I not suggest some
good form for giving expression to this state of things?
After a little reflection, I thought I could.

" I will speak," said I, " as if I were the hero, and then you can see how it will suit."

" Yes," said she, " but you must not forget that what you say should be very gradual."

I tried to be as gradual as I could, and to indicate by slow degrees the state of mind in which we wished our hero to be. As the indication became stronger and stronger, I thought it right to take Miss Vancouver's hand ; but to this she objected, because, as she said, it was more than indication, and besides, it prevented her from writing down what I said. We argued this point a little while without altering our position, and I asserted that the hand-holding only gave point and earnestness to the hero's remarks, which otherwise would not be so natural and true to life ; and' if she wanted to use her right hand, her left hand would do to hold. We made this change, and I proceeded with the hero's remarks.

There was in our *pension* a young German girl named Margarita. She was a handsome, plump maiden, and spoke English very well. There was another young lady, also a German, named Gretzel. She was a little creature and the fast friend of Margarita. These two had a companion whose name I did not know. She was a little older than the others, and was, I think, a Pole. She also understood English. As I was warming up toward the peroration of our hero's indication, I raised my eyes, and saw, on the brow of the hill, not a stone's throw from us, these three girls. They were talking earnestly and walking directly toward us. The place where they were was used as a public pleasure-ground, and was separated from the old court-yard by a pale-fence. Although the girls could not come to us, there was nothing to prevent their seeing us if they chose to look our way, for they were on ground which was higher than the top of the fence.

When I saw these girls, I was horror-stricken, and my knees, on which I rested, trembled beneath me. I did not dare to rise, nor to change my position, for fear the motion should attract attention; nor did I cease my remarks, for had I suddenly done so, my companion would have locked around to see what was the matter, and would certainly have jumped up, or have done something which would have brought the eyes of those girls upon us; but my voice dropped very low, and I wondered if there was any way of my gently rolling out of sight.

But at this moment our young man with a mystery suddenly appeared on the other side of the fence, walking rapidly toward the girls. There was something on the ocean, probably a ship, to which he directed their attention; and then he actually led them off, pointing, as it appeared, to a spot from which the distant object could be more plainly seen. They all walked away and disappeared behind the brow of the hill. With a great feeling of relief, I arose and recounted what had happened. Miss Vancouver sprang to her feet, shut up her blank-book, and put the stopper on her stylograph.

"This place will not do at all to work in," she said. "I will not have those girls staring at us."

I was obliged to admit that this particular spot would not do. I had not thought of any one walking in the grounds immediately above us, especially in the morning, which was our working time.

"They may return," she said, "and we must go away immediately and separately."

But I could not agree thus to give up our new-found study. The enclosure was quite extensive, with ruins at the other end, near which we might find some spot entirely protected from observation. So I went to look for such a place, leaving Miss Vancouver under the olive-tree, where, if she were seen alone, it would not matter. I found a spot which might answer, and, returning to the tree, sent her to look at it. While we were thus engaged, we heard the report of the noon cannon. This startled us both. The hour for *déjeûner à la fourchette* at the *pension* was twelve o'clock, and people were generally very prompt at that meal. It would not do for us to be late. Snatching up our effects, we hurried to the green door, but when I tried to open it as before, I found it impossible — a projecting strip of wood on the inside of the door-way preventing my reaching the bolt with my knife-blade. I tried to tear away the strip, but it was too firmly fastened. We both became very nervous and troubled. It was impossible to get out of the enclosure except through that door, for the wall was quite high and the top covered with broken glass embedded in the mortar. The party on the hill had had time to go down and around through the town to the *pension*. Our places at the table would be the only ones empty. What could attract more attention than this? And what would Mrs. Vancouver think and say?

At this moment we heard some one working at the lock on the other side. The door opened, and there stood our hero.

"I heard some one at this door," he said; "and supposing it had been accidentally closed, I came up and opened it."

"Thank you; thank you very much!" cried Miss Vancouver.

And away she ran to the house. If only I were late, it did not matter at all. I followed with our hero, and endeavored to make some explanation of the predicament of myself and the young lady. He took it all as a matter of course, as if the old court-yard were a place of general resort.

"When persons stroll through that door," he said, "they should put a piece of stick or of stone against the jamb, so that if the door is blown shut by the wind the latch may not catch."

And then he called my attention to a beautiful plant of the aloe kind which had just begun to blossom.

Miss Vancouver reached the breakfast-table in good time, but she told me afterward she would work in the old court-yard no more. The perils were too many.

For some days after this our story made little progress, for opportunities for consultation did not occur. I was particularly sorry for this, because I wanted very much to know how Miss Vancouver liked my indicative speech and what she had made of it. Early one afternoon about this time our hero, between whom and myself a slight acquaintance had sprung up, came to me and said:

"The sea is so perfectly smooth and quiet to-day that I thought it would be pleasant to take a row, and I have hired a boat. How would you like to go with me?"

I was pleased with his friendly proposition, and I am very fond of rowing; but yet I hesitated about accepting the invitation, for I hoped that afternoon to find some opportunity for consultation in regard to the work on which I was engaged.

"The boat is rather large for two persons," he remarked. "Have you any friends you would like to ask to go with us?"

This put a different phase upon affairs. I instantly said that I thought a row would be charming that afternoon, and suggested that Mrs. Vancouver and her daughter might like to take advantage of the opportunity.

The ladies were quite willing to go, and in twenty minutes we set off, two fishermen in red liberty caps pushing us from the pebbly beach. Our hero took one oar and I another, and we pulled together very well. The ladies sat in the stern, and enjoyed the smooth sea and the lovely day. We rowed across the little bay and around a high promontory, where there was a larger bay with a small town in the distance. The hero suggested that we should land here, as we could get some good views from the rocks. To this we all agreed; and when we had climbed up a little distance, Mrs. Vancouver found some wild flowers which interested her very much. She was, in a certain way, a floraphobist, and took an especial delight in finding in foreign countries blossoms which were the same as or similar to flowers she was familiar with in New England. Our hero had also a fancy for wild flowers, and it was not long before he showed Mrs. Vancouver a little blossom which she was very sure she had seen either at East Gresham or Milton Centre. Leaving these two to their floral researches, Miss Vancouver and I climbed higher up the rocks, where the view would be better. We found a pleasant ledge; and although we could not see what was going on below us, and the view was quite cut off in the direction of the town, we had an admirable outlook over the sea, on which, in the far distance, we could see the sails of a little vessel.

"This will be an admirable place to do a little work on our story," I said. "I have brought my blank-book and stylograph."

"And so have I," said she.

I then told her that I had been thinking over the matter a good deal, and that I believed in a short story two long speeches would be enough for the hero to make, and proposed that we should now go on with the second one. She thought well of that, and took a seat upon a rocky projection, while I sat upon another quite near.

"This second speech," said I, "ought to be more than indicative, and should express the definite purpose of the hero's sentiments; and I think there should be corresponding expressions from the heroine, and would be glad to have you suggest such as you think she would make." I then began to say what I thought a

hero ought to say under the circumstances. I soon
warmed up to my task wonderfully, and expressed
with much earnestness and ardor the sentiments I
thought proper for the occasion. I first held one of
Miss Vancouver's hands, and then both of them, she
trusting to her memory in regard to memoranda. Her
remarks in the character of the heroine were, however,
much briefer than mine, but they were enough. If
necessary, they could be worked up and amplified. I
think we had said all or nearly all there was to say
when we heard a shout from below. It was our hero
calling us. We could not see him, but I knew his
voice. He shouted again, and then I arose from the
rock on which Bessie was sitting and answered him.
He now made his appearance some distance below us,
and said that Mrs. Vancouver did not care to come up
any higher to get the views, and that she thought it
would be better to reach home before the sun should
set.

That evening, in the *salon*, Bessie spoke to me apart.
" Our hero," she said, " is more than a hero ; he is a
guardian angel. You must fathom his mystery. I
am sure that it is far better than any thing we can
invent for him."

I set myself to work to discover, if possible, not
only the mystery which had first interested us in our
hero, but also the reason and purpose of his guardian-
angelship. He was an American, and now that I had
come to know him better, I found him a very agreeable talker.

II.

Our hero was the first person whom I told of my engagement to Bessie. Mrs. Vancouver was very particular that this state of affairs should be made known. " If you are engaged," she said, " of course you can be together as much as you please. It is the custom in America, and nobody need make any remarks."

In talking to our hero, I told him of a good many little things that had happened at various times, and endeavored by these friendly confidences to make him speak of his own affairs. It must not be supposed that I was actuated by prying curiosity, but certainly I had a right to know something of a person to whom I had told so much; but he always seemed a great deal more interested in us than in himself, and I took so much interest in his interest, which was very kindly expressed, that his affairs never came into our conversation.

But just as he was going away, — he left the little town a few days before we did, — he told me that he was a writer, and that for some time past he had been engaged upon a story.

Our story was never finished. His was. This is it.

MR. TOLMAN.

MR. TOLMAN was a gentleman whose apparent age was of a varying character. At times, when deep in thought on business matters or other affairs, one might have thought him fifty-five or fifty-seven, or even sixty. Ordinarily, however, when things were running along in a satisfactory and commonplace way, he appeared to be about fifty years old, while upon some extraordinary occasions, when the world assumed an unusually attractive aspect, his age seemed to run down to forty-five or less.

He was the head of a business firm; in fact, he was the only member of it. The firm was known as Pusey and Co.; but Pusey had long been dead, and the " Co.," of which Mr. Tolman had been a member, was dissolved. Our elderly hero having bought out the business, firm name and all, for many years had carried it on with success and profit. His counting-house was a small and quiet place, but a great deal of money had been made in it. Mr. Tolman was rich — very rich indeed.

And yet as he sat in his counting-room one winter

evening he looked his oldest. He had on his hat and his overcoat, his gloves and his fur collar. Every one else in the establishment had gone home ; and he, with the keys in his hand, was ready to lock up and leave also. He often staid later than any one else, and left the keys with Mr. Canterfield, the head clerk, as he passed his house on his way home.

Mr. Tolman seemed in no hurry to go. He simply sat and thought, and increased his apparent age. The truth was he did not want to go home. He was tired of going home. This was not because his home was not a pleasant one. No single gentleman in the city had a handsomer or more comfortable suite of rooms. It was not because he felt lonely, or regretted that a wife and children did not brighten and enliven his home. He was perfectly satisfied to be a bachelor. The conditions suited him exactly. But, in spite of all this, he was tired of going home.

"I wish," said Mr. Tolman to himself, "that I could feel some interest in going home ; " and then he rose and took a turn or two up and down the room ; but as that did not seem to give him any more interest in the matter, he sat down again. "I wish it were neces-sary for me to go home," said he ; "but it isn't ; " and then he fell again to thinking. "What I need," he said, after a while, "is to depend more upon myself — to feel that I am necessary to myself. Just now I'm not. I'll stop going home — at least in this way. Where's the sense in envying other men, when I can have all that they have, just as well as not? And I'll have it, too," said Mr. Tolman, as he went out and locked the doors. Once in the streets, and walking rapidly, his ideas shaped themselves easily and readily into a plan which, by the time he reached the house of his head clerk, was quite matured. Mr. Canterfield was just going down to dinner as his employer rang the bell, so he opened the door himself. "I will detain you but a minute or two," said Mr. Tolman, handing the keys to Mr. Canterfield. "Shall we step into the parlor?"

When his employer had gone, and Mr. Canterfield had joined his family at the dinner table, his wife immediately asked him what Mr. Tolman wanted.

"Only to say that he is going away to-morrow, and that I am to attend to the business, and send his personal letters to ——," naming a city not a hundred miles away.

"How long is he going to stay?"

"He didn't say," answered Mr. Canterfield.

"I'll tell you what he ought to do," said the lady. "He ought to make you a partner in the firm, and then he could go away and stay as long as he pleased."

"He can do that now," returned her husband. "He has made a good many trips since I have been with him, and things have gone on very much in the same way as when he was here. He knows that."

"But still you'd like to be a partner?"

"Oh, yes," said Mr. Canterfield.

"And common gratitude ought to prompt him to make you one," said his wife.

Mr. Tolman went home and wrote a will. He left all his property, with the exception of a few legacies, to the richest and most powerful charitable organization in the country.

"People will think I'm crazy," said he to himself; "and if I should die while I am carrying out my plan, I'll leave the task of defending my sanity to people who are able to make a good fight for me." And before he went to bed he had his will signed and witnessed.

The next day he packed a trunk and left for the neighboring city. His apartments were to be kept in readiness for his return at any time. If you had seen him walking over to the railroad dépôt, you would have taken him for a man of forty-five.

When he arrived at his destination, Mr. Tolman established himself temporarily at a hotel, and spent the next three or four days in walking about the city looking for what he wanted. What he wanted was rather difficult to define, but the way in which he put the matter to himself was something like this:

"I'd like to find a snug little place where I can live and carry on some business which I can attend to myself, and which will bring me into contact with people of all sorts — people who will interest me. It must be a small business, because I don't want to have to work very hard, and it must be snug and comfortable, because I want to enjoy it. I would like a shop of some sort, because that brings a man face to face with his fellow-creatures."

The city in which he was walking about was one of the best places in the country in which to find the place of business he desired. It was full of independent little shops. But Mr. Tolman could not readily find

one which resembled his ideal. A small dry-goods establishment seemed to presuppose a female proprietor.
A grocery store would give him many interesting customers ; but he did not know much about groceries,
and the business did not appear to him to possess any
æsthetic features. He was much pleased by a small
shop belonging to a taxidermist. It was exceedingly
cosey, and the business was probably not so great as to
overwork any one. He might send the birds and beasts
which were brought to be stuffed to some practical
operator, and have him put them in proper condition
for the customers. He might — But no ; it would be
very unsatisfactory to engage in a business of which he
knew absolutely nothing. A taxidermist ought not to
blush with ignorance when asked some simple question
about a little dead bird or a defunct fish. And so he
tore himself from the window of this fascinating place,
where, he fancied, had his education been differently
managed, he could in time have shown the world the
spectacle of a cheerful and unblighted Mr. Venus.

The shop which at last appeared to suit him best
was one which he had passed and looked at several
times before it struck him favorably. It was in a small
brick house in a side street, but not far from one of the
main business avenues of the city. The shop seemed
devoted to articles of stationery and small notions of
various kinds not easy to be classified. He had stopped
to look at three penknives fastened to a card, which
was propped up in the little show-window, supported
on one side by a chess-board with " History of Asia " in
gilt letters on the back, and on the other by a small

violin labelled " 1 dollar ; " and as he gazed past these
articles into the interior of the shop, which was now
lighted up, it gradually dawned upon him that it was
something like his ideal of an attractive and interesting business place. At any rate he would go in and
look at it. He did not care for a violin, even at the low
price marked on the one in the window, but a new
pocket-knife might be useful ; so he walked in and
asked to look at pocket-knives.

The shop was in charge of a very pleasant old lady
of about sixty, who sat sewing behind the little counter. While she went to the window, and very carefully reached over the articles displayed therein to get
the card of penknives, Mr. Tolman looked about him.
The shop was quite small, but there seemed to be a
good deal in it. There were shelves behind the counter, and there were shelves on the opposite wall, and
they all seemed well filled with something or other.
In the corner near the old lady's chair was a little coal
stove with a bright fire in it, and at the back of the
shop, at the top of two steps, was a glass door partly
open, through which he saw a small room, with a red
carpet on the floor, and a little table apparently set
for a meal.

Mr. Tolman looked at the knives when the old lady
showed them to him, and after a good deal of consideration he selected one which he thought would be a
good knife to give to a boy. Then he looked over some
things in the way of paper-cutters, whist-markers, and
such small matters, which were in a glass case on the
counter ; and while he looked at them he talked to
the old lady.

She was a friendly, sociable body, and very glad to have any one to talk to, and so it was not at all difficult for Mr. Tolman, by some general remarks, to draw from her a great many points about herself and her shop. She was a widow, with a son who, from her remarks, must have been forty years old. He was connected with a mercantile establishment, and they had lived here for a long time. While her son was a salesman, and came home every evening, this was very pleasant ; but after he became a commercial traveller, and was away from the city for months at a time, she did not like it at all. It was very lonely for her.

Mr. Tolman's heart rose within him, but he did not interrupt her.

"If I could do it," said she, "I would give up this place, and go and live with my sister in the country. It would be better for both of us, and Henry could come there just as well as here when he gets back from his trips."

"Why don't you sell out?" asked Mr. Tolman, a little fearfully, for he began to think that all this was too easy sailing to be entirely safe.

"That would not be easy," said she, with a smile. "It might be a long time before we could find any one who would want to take the place. We have a fair trade in the store, but it isn't what it used to be when times were better; and the library is falling off too. Most of the books are getting pretty old, and it don't pay to spend much money for new ones now."

"The library!" said Mr. Tolman. "Have you a library?"

" Oh, yes," replied the old lady. " I've had a circulating library here for nearly fifteen years. There it is
on those two upper shelves behind you."

Mr. Tolman turned, and beheld two long rows of
books, in brown paper covers, with a short step-ladder
standing near the door of the inner room, by which
these shelves might be reached. This pleased him
greatly. He had had no idea that there was a library
here.

" I declare ! " said he. " It must be very pleasant
to manage a circulating library — a small one like this,
I mean. I shouldn't mind going into a business of the
kind myself."

The old lady looked up, surprised. Did he wish to
go into business ? She had not supposed that, just
from looking at him.

Mr. Tolman explained his views to her. He did not
tell what he had been doing in the way of business, or
what Mr. Canterfield was doing for him now. He
merely stated his present wishes, and acknowledged to
her that it was the attractiveness of her establishment
that had led him to come in.

" Then you do not want the penknife ? " she said,
quickly.

" Oh, yes, I do," said he ; " and I really believe, if
we can come to terms, that I would like the two other
knives, together with the rest of your stock in trade."

The old lady laughed a little nervously. She hoped
very much indeed that they could come to terms. She
brought a chair from the back room, and Mr. Tolman
sat down with her by the stove to talk it over. Few

customers came in to interrupt them, and they talked the matter over very thoroughly. They both came to the conclusion that there would be no difficulty about terms, nor about Mr. Tolman's ability to carry on the business after a very little instruction from the present proprietress. When Mr. Tolman left, it was with the understanding that he was to call again in a couple of days, when the son Henry would be at home, and matters could be definitely arranged.

When the three met, the bargain was soon struck. As each party was so desirous of making it, few difficulties were interposed. The old lady, indeed, was in favor of some delay in the transfer of the establishment, as she would like to clean and dust every shelf and corner and every article in the place ; but Mr. Tolman was in a hurry to take possession ; and as the son Henry would have to start off on another trip in a short time, he wanted to see his mother moved and settled before he left. There was not much to move but trunks and bandboxes, and some antiquated pieces of furniture of special value to the old lady, for Mr. Tolman insisted on buying every thing in the house, just as it stood. The whole thing did not cost him, he said to himself, as much as some of his acquaintances would pay for a horse. The methodical son Henry took an account of stock, and Mr. Tolman took several lessons from the old lady, in which she explained to him how to find out the selling prices of the various articles from the marks on the little tags attached to them ; and she particularly instructed him in the management of the circulating library. She informed him of the character of the books, and, as far as possible, of the character of the regular patrons. She told him whom he might trust to take out a book without paying for the one brought in, if they didn't happen to have the change with them, and she indicated with little crosses opposite their names those persons who should be required to pay cash down for what they had had, before receiving further benefits.

It was astonishing to see what interest Mr. Tolman took in all this. He was really anxious to meet some of the people about whom the old lady discoursed. He tried, too, to remember a few of the many things she told him of her methods of buying and selling, and the general management of her shop; and he probably did not forget more than three-fourths of what she told him.

Finally, every thing was settled to the satisfaction of the two male parties to the bargain — although the old lady thought of a hundred things she would yet like to do — and one fine frosty afternoon a car-load of furniture and baggage left the door, the old lady and her son took leave of the old place, and Mr. Tolman was left sitting behind the little counter, the sole manager and proprietor of a circulating library and a stationery and notion shop. He laughed when he thought of it, but he rubbed his hands and felt very well satisfied.

"There is nothing really crazy about it," he said to himself. "If there is a thing that I think I would like, and I can afford to have it, and there's no harm in it, why not have it?"

There was nobody there to say any thing against

this; so Mr. Tolman rubbed his hands again before the fire, and rose to walk up and down his shop, and wonder who would be his first customer.

In the course of twenty minutes a little boy opened the door and came in. Mr. Tolman hastened behind the counter to receive his commands. The little boy wanted two sheets of note-paper and an envelope.

"Any particular kind?" asked Mr. Tolman.

The boy didn't know of any particular variety being desired. He thought the same kind she always got would do; and he looked very hard at Mr. Tolman, evidently wondering at the change in the shop-keeper, but asking no questions.

"You are a regular customer, I suppose," said Mr. Tolman, opening several boxes of paper which he had taken down from the shelves. "I have just begun business here, and don't know what kind of paper you have been in the habit of buying. But I suppose this will do;" and he took out a couple of sheets of the best, with an envelope to match. These he carefully tied up in a piece of thin brown paper, and gave to the boy, who handed him three cents. Mr. Tolman took them, smiled, and then having made a rapid calculation, he called to the boy, who was just opening the door, and gave him back one cent.

"You have paid me too much," he said.

The boy took the cent, looked at Mr. Tolman, and then got out of the store as quickly as he could.

"Such profits as that are enormous," said Mr. Tolman; "but I suppose the small sales balance them." This Mr. Tolman subsequently found to be the case.

One or two other customers came in in the course of the afternoon, and about dark the people who took out books began to arrive. These kept Mr. Tolman very busy. He not only had to do a good deal of entering and cancelling, but he had to answer a great many questions about the change in proprietorship, and the probability of his getting in some new books, with suggestions as to the quantity and character of these, mingled with a few dissatisfied remarks in regard to the volumes already on hand.

Every one seemed sorry that the old lady had gone away; but Mr. Tolman was so pleasant and anxious to please, and took such an interest in their selection of books, that only one of the subscribers appeared to take the change very much to heart. This was a young man who was forty-three cents in arrears. He was a long time selecting a book, and when at last he brought it to Mr. Tolman to be entered, he told him in a low voice that he hoped there would be no objection to letting his account run on for a little while longer. On the first of the month he would settle it, and then he hoped to be able to pay cash whenever he brought in a book.

Mr. Tolman looked for his name on the old lady's list, and finding no cross against it, told him that it was all right, and that the first of the month would do very well. The young man went away perfectly satisfied with the new librarian. Thus did Mr. Tolman begin to build up his popularity. As the evening grew on he found himself becoming very hungry; but he did not like to shut up the shop, for every now and then some one dropped in, sometimes to ask what time it was, and sometimes to make a little purchase, while there were still some library patrons coming in at intervals.

However, taking courage during a short rest from customers, he put up the shutters, locked the door, and hurried off to a hotel, where he partook of a meal such as few keepers of little shops ever think of indulging in.

The next morning Mr. Tolman got his own breakfast. This was delightful. He had seen how cosily the old lady had spread her table in the little back room, where there was a stove suitable for any cooking he might wish to indulge in, and he longed for such a cosey meal. There were plenty of stock provisions in the house, which he had purchased with the rest of the goods; and he went out and bought himself a fresh loaf of bread. Then he broiled a piece of ham, made some good strong tea, boiled some eggs, and had a breakfast on the little round table, which, though plain enough, he enjoyed more than any breakfast at his club which he could remember. He had opened the shop, and sat facing the glass door, hoping, almost, that there would be some interruption to his meal. It would seem so much more proper in that sort of business if he had to get up and go attend to a customer.

Before evening of that day Mr. Tolman became convinced that he would soon be obliged to employ a boy or some one to attend to the establishment during his absence. After breakfast, a woman recommended by

the old lady came to make his bed and clean up generally, but when she had gone he was left alone with his
shop. He determined not to allow this responsibility
to injure his health, and so at one o'clock boldly locked
the shop door and went out to his lunch. He hoped
that no one would call during his absence, but when
he returned he found a little girl with a pitcher standing at the door. She came to borrow half a pint of
milk.

"Milk!" exclaimed Mr. Tolman, in surprise.
"Why, my child, I have no milk. I don't even use
it in my tea."

The little girl looked very much disappointed. "Is
Mrs. Walker gone away for good?" said she.

"Yes," replied Mr. Tolman. "But I would be
just as willing to lend you the milk as she would be, if
I had any. Is there any place near here where you
can buy milk?"

"Oh, yes," said the girl; "you can get it round in
the market-house."

"How much would half a pint cost?" he asked.

"Three cents," replied the girl.

"Well, then," said Mr. Tolman, "here are three
cents. You can go and buy the milk for me, and then
you can borrow it. Will that suit?"

The girl thought it would suit very well, and away
she went.

Even this little incident pleased Mr. Tolman. It
was so very novel. When he came back from his
dinner in the evening, he found two circulating library
subscribers stamping their feet on the door-step, and

he afterward heard that several others had called and gone away. It would certainly injure the library if he suspended business at meal-times. He could easily have his choice of a hundred boys if he chose to advertise for one, but he shrank from having a youngster in the place. It would interfere greatly with his cosiness and his experiences. He might possibly find a boy who went to school, and who would be willing to come at noon and in the evening if he were paid enough. But it would have to be a very steady and responsible boy. He would think it over before taking any steps.

He thought it over for a day or two, but he did not spend his whole time in doing so. When he had no customers, he sauntered about in the little parlor over the shop, with its odd old furniture, its quaint prints on the walls, and its absurd ornaments on the mantel-piece. The other little rooms seemed almost as funny to him, and he was sorry when the bell on the shop door called him down from their contemplation. It was pleasant to him to think that he owned all these odd things. The ownership of the varied goods in the shop also gave him an agreeable feeling, which none of his other possessions had ever afforded him. It was all so odd and novel.

He liked much to look over the books in the library. Many of them were old novels, the names of which were familiar enough to him, but which he had never read. He determined to read some of them as soon as he felt fixed and settled.

In looking over the book in which the names and accounts of the subscribers were entered, he amused himself by wondering what sort of persons they were who had out certain books. Who, for instance, wanted to read "The Book of Cats;" and who could possibly care for "The Mysteries of Udolpho?" But the unknown person in regard to whom Mr. Tolman felt the greatest curiosity was the subscriber who now had in his possession a volume entitled "Dormstock's Logarithms of the Diapason."

"How on earth," exclaimed Mr. Tolman, "did such a book get into this library; and where on earth did the person spring from who would want to take it out? And not only want to take it," he continued, as he examined the entry regarding the volume, "but come and have it renewed one, two, three, four — nine times! He has had that book for eighteen weeks!"

Without exactly making up his mind to do so, Mr. Tolman deferred taking steps toward getting an assistant until P. Glascow, the person in question, should make an appearance, and it was nearly time for the book to be brought in again.

"If I get a boy now," thought Mr. Tolman, "Glascow will be sure to come and bring the book while I am out."

In almost exactly two weeks from the date of the last renewal of the book, P. Glascow came in. It was the middle of the afternoon, and Mr. Tolman was alone. This investigator of musical philosophy was a quiet young man of about thirty, wearing a light brown cloak, and carrying under one arm a large book.

P. Glascow was surprised when he heard of the change in the proprietorship of the library. Still he hoped that there would be no objection to his renewing the book which he had with him, and which he had taken out some time ago.

"Oh, no," said Mr. Tolman, "none in the world. In fact, I don't suppose there are any other subscribers who would want it. I have had the curiosity to look to see if it had ever been taken out before, and I find it has not."

The young man smiled quietly. "No," said he, "I suppose not. It is not every one who would care to study the higher mathematics of music, especially when treated as Dormstock treats the subject."

"He seems to go into it pretty deeply," remarked Mr. Tolman, who had taken up the book. "At least I should think so, judging from all these calculations, and problems, and squares, and cubes."

"Indeed he does," said Glascow; "and although I have had the book some months, and have more reading time at my disposal than most persons, I have only reached the fifty-sixth page, and doubt if I shall not have to review some of that before I can feel that I thoroughly understand it."

"And there are three hundred and forty pages in all," said Mr. Tolman, compassionately.

"Yes," replied the other; "but I am quite sure that the matter will grow easier as I proceed. I have found that out from what I have already done."

"You say you have a good deal of leisure?" remarked Mr. Tolman. "Is the musical business dull at present?"

"Oh, I'm not in the musical business," said Glas-

cow. "I have a great love for music, and wish to
thoroughly understand it; but my business is quite
different. I am a night druggist, and that is the reason I have so much leisure for reading."

"A night druggist?" repeated Mr. Tolman, inquir-
ingly.

"Yes, sir," said the other. "I am in a large down-
town drug-store, which is kept open all night, and I go
on duty after the day-clerks leave."

"And does that give you more leisure?" asked Mr.
Tolman.

"It seems to," answered Glascow. "I sleep until
about noon, and then I have the rest of the day, until
seven o'clock, to myself. I think that people who
work at night can make a more satisfactory use of
their own time than those who work in the daytime.
In the summer I can take a trip on the river, or go
somewhere out of town, every day, if I like."

"Daylight is more available for many things, that is
true," said Mr. Tolman. "But is it not dreadfully
lonely sitting in a drug-store all night? There can't
be many people to come to buy medicine at night. I
thought there was generally a night-bell to drug-stores,
by which a clerk could be awakened if any body
wanted any thing."

"It's not very lonely in our store at night," said
Glascow. "In fact, it's often more lively then than in
the daytime. You see, we are right down among the
newspaper offices, and there's always somebody coming in for soda-water, or cigars, or something or other.
The store is a bright warm place for the night editors

and reporters to meet together and talk and drink hot soda, and there's always a knot of 'em around the stove about the time the papers begin to go to press. And they're a lively set, I can tell you, sir. I've heard some of the best stories I ever heard in my life told in our place after three o'clock in the morning."

"A strange life!" said Mr. Tolman. "Do you know, I never thought that people amused themselves in that way. And night after night, I suppose."

"Yes, sir, night after night, Sundays and all."

The night druggist now took up his book.

"Going home to read?" asked Mr. Tolman.

"Well, no," said the other; "it's rather cold this afternoon to read. I think I'll take a brisk walk."

"Can't you leave your book until you return?" asked Mr. Tolman; "that is, if you will come back this way. It's an awkward book to carry about."

"Thank you, I will," said Glascow. "I shall come back this way."

When he had gone, Mr. Tolman took up the book, and began to look over it more carefully than he had done before. But his examination did not last long.

"How anybody of common-sense can take any interest in this stuff is beyond my comprehension," said Mr. Tolman, as he closed the book and put it on a little shelf behind the counter.

When Glascow came back, Mr. Tolman asked him to stay and warm himself; and then, after they had talked for a short time, Mr. Tolman began to feel hungry. He had his winter appetite, and had lunched early. So said he to the night druggist, who had opened his " Dormstock," " How would you like to sit here and read a while, while I go and get my dinner? I will light the gas, and you can be very comfortable here, if you are not in a hurry."

P. Glascow was in no hurry at all, and was very glad to have some quiet reading by a warm fire ; and so Mr. Tolman left him, feeling perfectly confident that a man who had been allowed by the old lady to renew a book nine times must be perfectly trustworthy.

When Mr. Tolman returned, the two had some further conversation in the corner by the little stove.

" It must be rather annoying," said the night druggist, " not to be able to go out to your meals without shutting up your shop. If you like," said he, rather hesitatingly, " I will stop in about this time in the afternoon, and stay here while you go to dinner. I'll be glad to do this until you get an assistant. I can easily attend to most people who come in, and others can wait."

Mr. Tolman jumped at this proposition. It was exactly what he wanted.

So P. Glascow came every afternoon and read " Dormstock " while Mr. Tolman went to dinner ; and before long he came at lunch-time also. It was just as convenient as not, he said. He had finished his breakfast, and would like to read awhile. Mr. Tolman fancied that the night druggist's lodgings were, perhaps, not very well warmed, which idea explained the desire to walk rather than read on a cold afternoon. Glascow's name was entered on the free list, and he always took away the " Dormstock " at night, because he might have a chance of looking into it at the store, when custom began to grow slack in the latter part of the early morning.

One afternoon there came into the shop a young lady, who brought back two books which she had had for more than a month. She made no excuses for keeping the books longer than the prescribed time, but simply handed them in and paid her fine. Mr. Tolman did not like to take this money, for it was the first of the kind he had received ; but the young lady looked as if she was well able to afford the luxury of keeping books over their time, and business was business. So he gravely gave her her change. Then she said she would like to take out " Dormstock's Logarithms of the Diapason."

Mr. Tolman stared at her. She was a bright, handsome young lady, and looked as if she had very good sense. He could not understand it. But he told her the book was out.

" Out ! " she said. " Why, it's always out. It seems strange to me that there should be such a demand for that book. I have been trying to get it for ever so long."

" It *is* strange," said Mr. Tolman ; " but it is certainly in demand. Did Mrs. Walker ever make you any promises about it ? "

" No," said she ; " but I thought my turn would come around some time. And I particularly want the book just now."

Mr. Tolman felt somewhat troubled. He knew that the night druggist ought not to monopolize the volume, and yet he did not wish to disoblige one who was so useful to him, and who took such an earnest interest in the book. And he could not temporize with the young lady, and say that he thought the book would soon be in. He knew it would not. There were three hundred and forty pages of it. So he merely remarked that he was sorry.

" So am I." said the young lady, " very sorry. It so happens that just now 1 have a peculiar opportunity for studying that book, which may not occur again."

There was something in Mr. Tolman's sympathetic face which seemed to invite her confidence, and she continued.

" I am a teacher," she said, " and on account of certain circumstances I have a holiday for a month, which I intended to give up almost entirely to the study of music, and I particularly wanted " Dormstock." Do you think there is any chance of its early return, and will you reserve it for me? "

" Reserve it ! " said Mr. Tolman. " Most certainly I will." And then he reflected a second or two. " If you will come here the day after to-morrow, I will be able to tell you something definite."

She said she would come.

Mr. Tolman was out a long time at lunch-time the next day. He went to all the leading book-stores to see if he could buy a copy of Dormstock's great work. But he was unsuccessful. The booksellers told him that there was no probability that he could get a copy in the country, unless, indeed, he found it in the stock of some second-hand dealer. There was no demand

at all for it, and that if he even sent for it to England,
where it was published, it was not likely he could get
it, for it had been long out of print. The next day he
went to several second-hand stores, but no " Dormstock " could he find.

When he came back he spoke to Glascow on the
subject. He was sorry to do so, but thought that
simple justice compelled him to mention the matter.
The night druggist was thrown into a perturbed state
of mind by the information that some one wanted his
beloved book.

" A woman ! " he exclaimed. " Why, she would
not understand two pages out of the whole of it. It is
too bad. I didn't suppose any one would want this
book."

" Do not disturb yourself too much," said Mr. Tolman. " I am not sure that you ought to give it up."

" I am very glad to hear you say so," said Glascow.
" I have no doubt it is only a passing fancy with her.
I dare say she would really rather have a good new
novel : " and then, having heard that the lady was
expected that afternoon, he went out to walk, with the
" Dormstock " under his arm.

When the young lady arrived, an hour or so later,
she was not at all satisfied to take out a new novel,
and was very sorry indeed not to find the " Logarithms
of the Diapason " waiting for her. Mr. Tolman told
her that he had tried to buy another copy of the work,
and for this she expressed herself gratefully. He also
found himself compelled to say that the book was in
the possession of a gentleman who had had it for some

time — all the time it had been out, in fact — and had not yet finished it.

At this the young lady seemed somewhat nettled.

"Is it not against the rules for any person to keep one book out so long?" she asked.

"No," said Mr. Tolman. "I have looked into that. Our rules are very simple, and merely say that a book may be renewed by the payment of a certain sum."

"Then I am never to have it?" remarked the young lady.

"Oh, I wouldn't despair about it," said Mr. Tolman. "He has not had time to reflect upon the matter. He is a reasonable young man, and I believe that he will be willing to give up his study of the book for a time and let you take it."

"No," said she, "I don't wish that. If he is studying, as you say he is, day and night, I do not wish to interrupt him. I should want the book at least a month, and that, I suppose, would upset his course of study entirely. But I do not think any one should begin in a circulating library to study a book that will take him a year to finish; for, from what you say, it will take this gentleman at least that time to finish Dormstock's book." And so she went her way.

When P. Glascow heard all this in the evening, he was very grave. He had evidently been reflecting.

"It is not fair," said he. "I ought not to keep the book so long. I now give it up for a while. You may let her have it when she comes." And he put the "Dormstock" on the counter, and went and sat down by the stove.

Mr. Tolman was grieved. He knew the night druggist had done right, but still he was sorry for him.
" What will you do?" he asked. " Will you stop
your studies?"

" Oh, no," said Glascow, gazing solemnly into the
stove. " I will take up some other books on the diapason which I have, and will so keep my ideas fresh
on the subject until this lady is done with the book.
I do not really believe she will study it very long."
And then he added: " If it is all the same to you, I
will come around here and read, as I have been doing,
until you shall get a regular assistant."

Mr. Tolman would be delighted to have him come,
he said. He had entirely given up the idea of getting
an assistant; but this he did not say.

It was some time before the lady came back, and
Mr. Tolman was afraid she was not coming at all.
But she did come, and asked for Mrs. Burney's " Evelina." She smiled when she named the book. and said
that she believed she would have to take a novel after
all, and she had always wanted to read that one.

" I wouldn't take a novel if I were you," said Mr.
Tolman; and he triumphantly took down the " Dormstock " and laid it before her.

She was evidently much pleased, but when he told
her of Mr. Glascow's gentlemanly conduct in the matter, her countenance instantly changed.

" Not at all," said she, laying down the book; " I
will not break up his study. I will take the ' Evelina,'
if you please."

And as no persuasion from Mr. Tolman had any

effect upon her, she went away with Mrs. Burney's novel in her muff.

" Now, then," said Mr. Tolman to Glascow, in the evening, " you may as well take the book along with you. She won't have it."

But Glascow would do nothing of the kind. " No," he remarked, as he sat looking into the stove ; " when I said I would let her have it, I meant it. She'll take it when she sees that it continues to remain in the library."

Glascow was mistaken : she did not take it, having the idea that he would soon conclude that it would be wiser for him to read it than to let it stand idly on the shelf.

" It would serve them both right," said Mr. Tolman to himself, " if somebody else would come and take it." But there was no one else among his subscribers who would even think of such a thing.

One day, however, the young lady came in and asked to look at the book. " Don't think that I am going to take it out," she said, noticing Mr. Tolman's look of pleasure as he handed her the volume. " I only wish to see what he says on a certain subject which I am studying now ; " and so she sat down by the stove, on the chair which Mr. Tolman placed for her, and opened " Dormstock."

She sat earnestly poring over the book for half an hour or more, and then she looked up and said, " I really cannot make out what this part means. Excuse my troubling you, but I would be very glad if you would explain the latter part of this passage."

"Me!" exclaimed Mr. Tolman: "why, my good madam — miss, I mean — I couldn't explain it to you if it were to save my life. But what page is it?" said he, looking at his watch.

" Page twenty-four," answered the young lady.

"Oh, well, then," said he, " if you can wait ten or fifteen minutes, the gentleman who has had the book will be here, and I think he can explain any thing in the first part of the work."

The young lady seemed to hesitate whether to wait or not; but as she had a certain curiosity to see what sort of a person he was who had been so absorbed in the book, she concluded to sit a little longer and look into some other parts of the book.

The night druggist soon came in; and when Mr. Tolman introduced him to the lady, he readily agreed to explain the passage to her if he could. So Mr. Tolman got him a chair from the inner room, and he also sat down by the stove.

The explanation was difficult, but it was achieved at last; and then the young lady broached the subject of leaving the book unused. This was discussed for some time, but came to nothing, although Mr. Tolman put down his afternoon paper and joined in the argument, urging, among other points, that as the matter now stood he was deprived by the dead-lock of all income from the book. But even this strong argument proved of no avail.

"Then I'll tell you what I wish you would do," said Mr. Tolman, as the young lady rose to go: "come here and look at the book whenever you wish to do so.

I'd like to make this more of a reading-room anyway. It would give me more company."

After this the young lady looked into "Dormstock" when she came in ; and as her holidays had been extended by the continued absence of the family in which she taught, she had plenty of time for study, and came quite frequently. She often met with Glascow in the shop ; and on such occasions they generally consulted "Dormstock," and sometimes had quite lengthy talks on musical matters. One afternoon they came in together, having met on their way to the library, and entered into a conversation on diapasonic logarithms, which continued during the lady's stay in the shop.

"The proper thing," thought Mr. Tolman, "would be for these two people to get married. Then they could take the book and study it to their hearts' content. And they would certainly suit each other, for they are both greatly attached to musical mathematics and philosophy, and neither of them either plays or sings, as they have told me. It would be an admirable match."

Mr. Tolman thought over this matter a good deal, and at last determined to mention it to Glascow. When he did so, the young man colored, and expressed the opinion that it would be of no use to think of such a thing. But it was evident from his manner and subsequent discourse that he had thought of it.

Mr. Tolman gradually became quite anxious on the subject, especially as the night druggist did not seem inclined to take any steps in the matter. The weather was now beginning to be warmer, and Mr. Tolman

reflected that the little house and the little shop were
probably much more cosey and comfortable in winter
than in summer.   There were higher buildings all about
the house, and even now he began to feel that the cir-
culation of air would be quite as agreeable as the circu-
lation of books.   He thought a good deal about his
airy rooms in the neighboring city.

"Mr. Glascow." said he, one afternoon, "I have
made up my mind to shortly sell out this business."

"What!" exclaimed the other.   "Do you mean
you will give it up and go away — leave the place altogether?"

"Yes," replied Mr. Tolman, "I shall give up the
place entirely, and leave the city."

The night druggist was shocked.   He had spent
many happy hours in that shop, and his hours there
were now becoming pleasanter than ever.   If Mr. Tolman went away, all this must end.   Nothing of the
kind could be expected of any new proprietor.

"And considering this," continued Mr. Tolman, "I
think it would be well for you to bring your love matters to a conclusion while I am here to help you."

"My love matters!" exclaimed Mr. Glascow, with
a flush.

"Yes, certainly," said Mr. Tolman.   "I have eyes,
and I know all about it.   Now let me tell you what I
think.   When a thing is to be done, it ought to be done
the first time there is a good chance.   That's the way
I do business.   Now you might as well come around
here to-morrow afternoon, prepared to propose to Miss
Edwards.   She is due to-morrow, for she has been two

days away. If she don't come, we'll postpone the matter until the next day. But you should be ready to-morrow. I don't believe you can see her much when you don't meet her here; for that family is expected back very soon, and from what I infer from her account of her employers, you won't care to visit her at their house.''

The night druggist wanted to think about it.

''There is nothing to think,'' said Mr. Tolman. ''We know all about the lady.'' (He spoke truly, for he had informed himself about both parties to the affair.) ''Take my advice, and be here to-morrow afternoon — and come rather early.''

The next morning Mr. Tolman went up to his parlor on the second floor, and brought down two blue stuffed chairs, the best he had, and put them in the little room back of the shop. He also brought down one or two knicknacks and put them on the mantel-piece, and he dusted and brightened up the room as well as he could. He even covered the table with a red cloth from the parlor.

When the young lady arrived, he invited her to walk into the back room to look over some new books he had just got in. If she had known he proposed to give up the business, she would have thought it rather strange that he should be buying new books. But she knew nothing of his intentions. When she was seated at the table whereon the new books were spread, Mr. Tolman stepped outside of the shop door to watch for Glascow's approach. He soon appeared.

''Walk right in,'' said Mr. Tolman. ''She's in the

back room looking over books. I'll wait here, and keep out customers as far as possible. It's pleasant, and I want a little fresh air. I'll give you twenty minutes."

Glascow was pale, but he went in without a word; and Mr. Tolman, with his hands under his coat-tail, and his feet rather far apart, established a blockade on the door-step. He stood there for some time looking at the people outside, and wondering what the people inside were doing. The little girl who had borrowed the milk of him, and who had never returned it, was about to pass the door; but seeing him standing there, she crossed over to the other side of the street. But he did not notice her. He was wondering if it was time to go in. A boy came up to the door, and wanted to know if he kept Easter-eggs. Mr. Tolman was happy to say he did not. When he had allowed the night druggist a very liberal twenty minutes, he went in. As he entered the shop door, giving the bell a very decided ring as he did so, P. Glascow came down the two steps that led from the inner room. His face showed that it was all right with him.

A few days after this, Mr. Tolman sold out his stock, good-will, and fixtures, together with the furniture and lease of the house. And who should he sell out to but to Mr. Glascow! This piece of business was one of the happiest points in the whole affair. There was no reason why the happy couple should not be married very soon, and the young lady was charmed to give up her position as teacher and governess in a family, and come and take charge of that delightful little store and that cunning little house, with almost every thing in it that they wanted.

One thing in the establishment Mr. Tolman refused to sell. That was Dormstock's great work. He made the couple a present of the volume, and between two of the earlier pages he placed a bank-note, which in value was very much more than that of the ordinary wedding-gift.

"And what are *you* going to do?" they asked of him, when all these things were settled. And then he told them how he was going back to his business in the neighboring city, and he told them what it was, and how he had come to manage a circulating library. They did not think him crazy. People who studied the logarithms of the diapason would not be apt to think a man crazy for such a little thing as that.

When Mr. Tolman returned to the establishment of Pusey & Co., he found every thing going on very satisfactorily.

"You look ten years younger, sir," said Mr. Canterfield. "You must have had a very pleasant time. I did not think there was enough to interest you in —— for so long a time."

"Interest me!" exclaimed Mr. Tolman. "Why, objects of interest crowded on me. I never had a more enjoyable holiday in my life."

When he went home that evening (and he found himself quite willing to go), he tore up the will he had made. He now felt that there was no necessity for proving his sanity.

ON THE TRAINING OF PARENTS.

FORTY or fifty years ago, when the middle-aged and old people of the present day were children or young people, the parent occupied a position in the family so entirely different from that in which we find him to-day, that the subject of his training was not perhaps of sufficient importance to receive attention from those engaged in the promotion of education. The training of the child by the parent, both as a necessary element in the formation of its character and as a preparation for its education in the schools, was then considered the only branch of family instruction and discipline to which the thought and the assistance of workers in social reform should be given.

But now that there has been such a change, especially in the United States, in the constitution of the family, when the child has taken into its own hands that authority which was once the prerogative of the parent, it is time that we should recognize the altered condition of things, and give to the children of the present day that assistance and counsel in the government and judicious training of their parents which was

166

once so freely offered to the latter when their offspring held a subordinate position in the family and household.

Since this radical change in the organization of the family a great responsibility has fallen upon the child; it finds itself in a position far more difficult than that previously held by the parent. It has upon its hands not a young and tender being, with mind unformed and disposition capable, in ordinary cases, of being easily moulded and directed, but two persons with minds and dispositions matured, and often set and hardened, whose currents of thought run in such well-worn channels, and whose judgments are so biased and prejudiced in favor of this or that line of conduct, that the labor and annoyance of their proper training is frequently evaded, and the parents are remanded to the position of providers of necessities, without any effort on the part of the child to assist them to adapt themselves to their new condition.

Not only has the child of the present day the obvious difficulties of its position to contend with, but it has no traditions to fall back upon for counsel and support. The condition of family affairs under consideration did not exist to any considerable extent before the middle of the present century, and there are no available records of the government of the parent by the child. Neither can it look to other parts of the world for examples of successful filial administration. Nowhere but in our own country can this state of things be said to prevail. It is necessary, therefore, that those who are able to do so should step forward in aid of the child as they formerly aided the parent, and see to it, as far as possible, that the latter receives the training which will enable him properly to perform the duties of the novel position which he has been called upon to fill. It is an injustice to millions of our citizens that the literature of the country contains nothing on this subject.

Whether it be done properly or improperly, the training of which we speak generally begins about the fifth or sixth year of parentage, although in cases where there happens to be but one trainer it often begins much earlier; but in these first years of filial rule the discipline is necessarily irregular and spasmodic, and it is not until the fourteenth or fifteenth year of his parental life that a man is generally enabled to understand what is expected of him by his offspring, and what line of conduct he must pursue in order to meet their views. It is, therefore, to the young people who have lived beyond their first decade that the great work of parent-training really belongs, and it is to them that we should offer our suggestions and advice.

It should be considered that this revolution in the government of the family was not one of force. The father and the mother were not hurled from their position and authority by the superior power of the child, but these positions have been willingly abdicated by the former, and promptly and unhesitatingly accepted by the latter. To the child then belongs none of the rights of the conqueror. Its subjects have voluntarily placed themselves under its rule, and by this act they have acquired a right to consideration and kindly sympathy which should never be forgotten by their youthful preceptors and directors. In his present position the parent has not only much to learn, but much to unlearn ; and while the child is endeavoring to indicate to him the path in which he should walk, it should remember that the feet of father or mother are often entirely unaccustomed to the peculiar pedestrianism now imposed upon them, and that allowance should be made for the frequent slips, and trips, and even falls, which may happen to them. There is but little doubt that severity is too frequently used in the education of parents. More is expected of them than should be expected of any class of people whose duties and obligations have never been systematically defined and codified. The parent who may be most anxious to fulfil the wishes of his offspring, and conduct himself in such manner as will meet the entire approval of the child, must often grope in the dark. It is therefore not only necessary to the peace and tranquillity of the family that his duties should be defined as clearly as possible, but this assistance is due to him as a mark of that filial affection which should not be permitted entirely to die out, simply because the parent has voluntarily assumed a position of inferiority and subjection. It is obvious, then, that it is the duty of the child to find out what it really wants, and then to make these wants clear and distinct to the parents. How many instances there are of fathers and mothers who spend hours, days, and even longer periods, in endeavoring to discover what it is that will satisfy the cravings of their child, and give them that position in its esteem which they are so desirous to hold. This is asking too much of the parent, and there are few whose mental vigor will long hold out when they are subjected, not only to the performance of onerous duties, but to the anxiety and vexation consequent upon the difficult task of discovering what those duties are.

Among the most forcible reasons why the rule of the child over the parent should be tempered by kind consideration, is the high degree of respect and deference now paid to the wants and opinions of children. In this regard they have absolutely nothing to complain of. The parent lives for the benefit of the child. In many cases the prosperity and happiness of the latter appears to be the sole reason for the existence of the former. How necessary is it, then, that persons occupying the position of parents in the prevalent organization of the family should not be left to exhaust themselves in undirected efforts, but that the development of their ability and power to properly perform the duties of the father and mother of the new era should be made the subject of the earnest thought and attention of the child.

It is difficult for those whose youth elapsed before the revolution in the family, and who, therefore, never enjoyed opportunities of exercising the faculties necessary in the government of parents, to give suitable advice and suggestion to those now engaged in this great work; but the following remarks are offered in the belief that they will receive due consideration from those to whom they are addressed.

There can be no doubt that it is of prime importance

in the training of a parent by the child that the matter should be taken in hand as early as possible. He or she who begins to feel, in the first years of parental life, the restrictions of filial control, will be much less difficult to manage as time goes on, than one who has not been made aware, until he has been a parent for perhaps ten or twelve years, that he is expected to shape his conduct in accordance with the wishes of his offspring. In such cases, habits of self-consideration, and even those of obtrusive self-assertion, are easily acquired by the parent, and are very difficult to break up. The child then encounters obstacles and discouragements which would not have existed had the discipline been begun when the mind of a parent was in a pliant and mouldable condition. Instances have occurred, when, on account of the intractable nature of father or mother. the education intended by the child has been entirely abandoned, and the parents allowed to take matters into their own hands, and govern the family as it used to be done before the new system came into vogue. But it will nearly always be found to be the case, in such instances, that the ideas of the parent concerning his rights and prerogatives in the family have been allowed to grow and take root to an extent entirely incompatible with easy removal.

The neglect of early opportunities of assuming control by the child who first enables a married couple to call themselves parents, is not only often detrimental to its own chances of holding the domestic reins, but it also trammels, to a great extent, the action of succeeding children. But no youngster, no matter how many brothers and sisters may have preceded it, or to what extent these may have allowed the parents to have their own way, need ever despair of assuming the control which the others have allowed to elude their grasp. It is not at all uncommon for the youngest child of a large family to be able to step to the front, and show to the others how a parent may be guided and regulated by the exercise of firm will and determined action.

If, as has been asserted, parental training is begun early enough, the child will find its task an easy one, and little advice will be needed by it, but in the case of delayed action there is one point which should be kept in mind, and that is that sudden and violent measures should, as far as possible, be avoided. In times gone by it used to be the custom of many parents, when offended by a child, to administer a box to the culprit's ear. An unexpected incident of this kind was apt to cause a sudden and tremendous change in the mental action of the young person boxed. His views of life; his recollections of the past; his aspirations for the future; his ideas of nature, of art, of the pursuit of happiness — were all merged and blended into one overwhelming sensation. For the moment he knew nothing on earth but the fact that he had been boxed. From this point the comprehension of his own status among created things; his understanding of surrounding circumstances, and of cosmic entities in general, had to begin anew. Whether he continued to be the same boy as before, or diverging one way or the other, became a better or a worse one, was a result not to be predetermined by any known process. Now it is not to be supposed that any ordinary child will undertake to box the ears of an ordinary parent, for the result in such a case might interfere with the whole course of training then in progress, but there is a mental box, quite as sudden in its action, and as astounding in its effect upon the boxee, as an actual physical blow, and it is no uncommon thing for a child to administer such a form of correction. But the practice is now as dangerous as it used to be, and as uncertain of good result, and it is earnestly urged upon the youth of the age to abolish it altogether. If a parent cannot be turned from the error of his ways by any other means than by a shock of this kind, it would be better, if the thing be possible, to give him into the charge of some children other than his own, and let them see what they can do with him.

We do not propose to liken a human parent to an animal so unintelligent as a horse ; but there are times when a child would find it to his advantage, and to that of his progenitor, to treat the latter in the same manner as a sensible and considerate man treats a nervous horse. An animal of this kind, when he sees by the roadside an obtrusive object with which he is not acquainted, is apt to imagine it a direful and ferocious creature, such as used to pounce upon his prehistoric ancestors ; and to refuse to approach its dangerous vicinity. Thereupon the man in charge of the horse, if he be a person of the character mentioned above, does not whip or spur the frightened animal until he rushes madly past the terrifying illusion, but quieting him by gentle word and action, leads him up to the object, and shows him that it is not a savage beast, eager for horseflesh, but an empty barrel, and that the fierce eye that he believed to be glaring upon him is nothing but the handle of a shovel protruding above the top. Then the horse, if there is any good in him, will be content to walk by that barrel; and the next time he sees it will be likely to pass it with perhaps but a hasty glance or two to see that its nature has not changed; and, in time, he will learn that barrels, and other things that he may not have noticed before, are not ravenous, and so become a better, because a wiser, horse. We know well that there are parents who, plodding along as quietly as any son or daughter could desire, will suddenly stop short at the sight of something thoroughly understood, and not at all disapproved of by his offspring, but which to him appears as objectionable and dangerous as the empty barrel to the high-strung horse. Now let not the youngster apply the mental lash, and urge that startled and reluctant parent forward. Better far if it take him figuratively by the bridle, and make him understand that that which appeared to him a vision of mental or physical ruin to a young person, or a frightful obstacle in the way of rational progress, is nothing but a pleasant form of intellectual recreation, which all persons ought to like very much, or to which, at least, they should have no objections. How many such phantasms will arise before a parent, and how necessary is it for a child, if it wish to carry on without disturbance its work of training, to get that parent into the habit of thinking that these things are really nothing but phantasms!

When it becomes necessary to punish a parent, no child should forget the importance of tempering severity with mercy. The methods in use in the by-gone times when the present condition of things was reversed, were generally of a physical nature, such as castigation, partial starvation, and restrictions in the pursuit of happiness, but those now inflicted by the children, acting upon the mental nature of the parents, are so severe and hard to bear that they should be used but sparingly. Not only is there danger that by undue severity an immediate progenitor may be permanently injured, and rendered of little value to himself and others, but there is sometimes a re-action, violent and sudden, and a family is forced to gaze upon the fearful spectacle of a parent at bay!

The tendency of a great portion of the youth, who have taken the governing power into their own hands, is to make but little use of it, and to allow their parents to go their own way, while they go upon theirs. Such neglect, however, cannot but be prejudicial to the permanency and force of the child-power. While the young person is pursuing a course entirely satisfactory to himself, doing what he likes, and leaving undone what he does not like, the unnoticed parent may be concocting schemes of domestic management entirely incompatible with the desires and plans of his offspring, and quietly building up obstacles which will be very difficult to overthrow when the latter shall have observed their existence. Eternal vigilance is not only the price of liberty, but it is also the price of supremacy. To keep one's self above another it is necessary to be careful to keep that other down. The practice of some fathers and mothers of coming frequently to the front, when their presence there is least expected or desired, must have been noticed by many children who had supposed their parents so thoroughly trained that they would not think of such a thing as causing trouble and annoyance to those above them. A parent is human, and cannot be depended upon to preserve always the same line of action ; and the children who are accustomed to see their fathers and mothers perfectly obedient, docile, and inoffensive, must not expect that satisfactory conduct to continue if they are allowed to discover that a guiding and controlling hand is not always upon them. There are parents, of course, who never desire to rise, even temporarily, from the inferior positions which, at the earliest possible period, they have assumed in their families. Such persons are perfectly safe ; and when a child perceives by careful observation that a parent belongs to this class, it may, without fear, relax much of the watchfulness and discipline necessary in most families, and content itself with merely indicating the path that it is desirable the elder person should pursue. Such parents are invaluable boons to an ambitious, energetic, and masterful child ; and if there were more of them the anxieties, the perplexities, and the difficulties of the child-power among us would be greatly ameliorated.

Even when parents may be considered to be conducting themselves properly, and to need no increase of vigilant control, it is often well for the child to enter into their pursuits ; to see what they are doing, and, if it should seem best, to help them do it. Of course, the parents are expected to promote and maintain the material interests of the family ; and as their labor, beyond that necessary for present necessities, is generally undertaken for the future benefit of the child, it is but fair that the latter should have something to say about this labor. In the majority of cases, however, the parent may, in this respect, safely be let alone. The more he gives himself up to the amassing of a competency, or a fortune, the less will he be likely to interfere with the purposes and actions of his children.

One of the most important results in the training under consideration is its influence upon the trainer. When a child has reduced its parents to a condition of docile obedience, and sees them day by day, and year by year, pursuing a path of cheerful subservience, it can scarcely fail to appreciate what will be expected of it when it shall itself have become a parent. Such observation, if accompanied by accordant reflection, cannot fail to make easier the rule of the coming child ; and, in conclusion, we would say to the children of the present day : Train up a parent in the way he should go, and when you are old you will know how to go that way yourself.

OUR FIRE-SCREEN.

IT was a fire-screen, — that is, it was a frame for one, — and it was made of ash. My wife had worked a very pretty square of silk, with flowers and other colored objects upon it; and when it was finished she thought she would use it for a fire-screen, and asked me to have a frame made for it. I ordered the frame of ash, because the cabinet-maker said that that was the fashionable wood at present; and when it came home my wife and I both liked it very much, although we could not help thinking that it ought to be painted. It was well made, — you could see the construction everywhere. One part ran through another part, and the ends were fastened with pegs. It was modelled, so the cabinet-maker informed me, in the regular Eastlake style.

It was a pretty frame, but the wood was of too light a color. It stared out at us from the midst of the other furniture. Of course it might be stained, and so made to harmonize with the rest of our sitting-room; but what would be the good of having it of ash if it were painted over? It might as well be of pine.

178

However, at my wife's suggestion, I got a couple of Eastlake chairs, also ash ; and with these at each side of the fire-place, the screen looked much better. The chairs were very well made, and would last a long time, especially, my wife said, as no one would care to sit down in them. They were, certainly, rather stiff and uncomfortable, but that was owing to the Eastlake pattern ; and as we did not need to use them, this was of no importance to us. Our house was furnished very comfortably. We made a point of having easy-chairs for our visitors as well as ourselves, and in fact, every thing about our house was easy, warm and bright. We believed that home should be a place of rest ; and we bought chairs and sofas and lounges which took you in their arms like a mother, and made you forget the toils of the world.

But we really did not enjoy the screen as much as we expected we should, and as much as we had enjoyed almost every thing that we had before bought for our house. Even with the companionship of the chairs, it did not seem to fit into the room. And every thing else fitted. I think I may honestly say that we were people of taste, and that there were few incongruities in our house-furnishing.

But the two chairs and the screen did not look like any thing else we had. They made our cosey sitting-room uncomfortable. We bore it as long as we could, and then we determined to take a bold step. We had always been consistent and thorough ; we would be so now. So we had all the furniture of the room removed, excepting the fire-screen and the two chairs, and replaced it with articles of the Eastlake style, in ash and oak. Of course our bright Wilton carpet did not suit these things, and we took it up, and had the floor puttied and stained and bought a Turko-Persian carpet that was only partly large enough for the room. The walls we re-papered, so as to tone them down to the general stiffness, and we had the ceiling colored sage-green, which would be in admirable keeping, the decorating man said.

We didn't like this room, but we thought we would try and learn to like it. The fault was in ourselves perhaps. High art in furniture was something we ought to understand and ought to like. We would do both if we could.

But we soon saw that one reason why we did not like our sitting-room was the great dissimilarity between it and the rest of the house. To come from our comfortable bedroom, or our handsome, bright and softly furnished parlor, or our cheerful dining-room, into this severe and middle-aged sitting-room was too great a rise (or fall) for our perceptions. The strain or the shock was injurious to us. So we determined to strike another blow in the cause of consistency. We would furnish our whole house in the Eastlake style.

Fortunately, my wife's brother had recently married, and had bought a house about a quarter of a mile from our place. He had, so far, purchased but little furniture, and when we refurnished our sitting-room, he took the old furniture at a moderate price, for which I was very glad, for I had no place to put it. I call it "old" furniture to distinguish it from the new; but in reality, it had not been used very long, and was in admirable condition. After buying these things from us, Tom — my brother-in-law — seemed to come to a stop in his house-furnishing. He and his wife lived in one or two rooms of their house, and appeared to be in no hurry to get themselves fixed and settled. Tom often came over and made remarks about our sitting-room, and the curious appearance it presented in the midst of a house furnished luxuriously in the most modern style ; and this helped us to come to the determination to Eastlake our house, thoroughly and completely.

Of course, as most of our new furniture had to be made to order, we could make our changes but slowly, and so refurnished one room at a time. Whenever a load of new furniture was brought to the house Tom was on hand to buy the things we had been using. I must say that he was very honorable about the price, for he always brought a second-hand-furniture man from the city, and made him value the things, and he then paid me according to this valuation. I was frequently very much surprised at the low estimates placed on articles for which I had paid a good deal of money, but of course I could not expect more than the regular second-hand-market price. He brought a different man every time ; and their estimates were all low, in about the same proportion, so I could not complain. I do not think he used the men well, however, for I found out afterward that they thought that he wanted to sell the goods to them.

Tom was a nice fellow, of course, because he was

my wife's brother, but there were some things about
him I did not like. He annoyed me a good deal by
coming around to our house, after it was newly furnished, and making remarks about the things.

"I can't see the sense," he said, one day, "in imi-
tating furniture that was made in the days when people
didn't know how to make furniture."

"Didn't know how!" I exclaimed. "Why, those
were just the days when they *did* know how. Look at
that bedstead! Did you ever see any thing more solid
and stanch and thoroughly honest than that? It will
last for centuries and always be what you see it now,
a strong, good, ash bedstead."

"That's the mischief of it," Tom answered. "It
will always be what it is now. If there was any chance
of its improving I'd like it better. I don't know exactly what you mean by an honest bedstead, but if it's
one that a fellow wouldn't wish to lie in, perhaps you're
right. And what do you want with furniture that will
last for centuries? You won't last for centuries, so
what difference can it make to you?"

"Difference enough," I answered. "I want none
of your flimsy modern furniture. I want well-made
things, in which the construction is first-class and evident. Look at that chair, for instance; you can see
just how it is put together."

"Exactly so," replied Tom, "but what's the good
of having one part of a chair run through another part
and fastened with a peg, so that its construction may
be evident?. If those old fellows in the Middle Ages
had known how to put chairs together as neatly and

strongly as some of our modern furniture, — such as mine, for instance, which you know well enough is just as strong as any furniture need be, — don't you suppose they would have done it? Of course they would. The trouble about the construction of a chair like that is that it makes your own construction too evident. When I sit in one of them I think I know exactly where my joints are put together, especially those in my back."

Tom seemed particularly to dislike the tiles that were set in many articles of my new furniture. He could not see what was the good of inserting crockery into bedsteads and writing-desks; and as to the old pictures on the tiles, he utterly despised them.

"If the old buffers who made the originals of those pictures," he said, "had known that free and enlightened citizens of the nineteenth century were going to copy them they'd have learned to draw."

However, we didn't mind this talk very much, and we even managed to smile when he made fun and puns and said:

"Well, I suppose people in your station are bound to do this thing, as it certainly is stylish." But.there was one thing he said that did trouble us. He came into the house one morning, and remarked:

"I don't want to make you dissatisfied with your new furniture, but it seems to me — and to other people, too, for I've heard them talking about it — that such furniture never can look as it ought to in such a house. In old times, when the people didn't know how to make any better furniture than this, they didn't know how to build decent houses either. They had no

plate-glass windows, or high ceilings, or hot and cold
water in every room, or stationary wash-tubs, or any
of that sort of thing.   They had small windows with
little panes of glass set in lead, and they had low
rooms with often no ceiling at all, so that you could
see the construction of the floor overhead, and they
had all the old inconveniences that we have cast aside.
If you want your furniture to look like what it makes
believe to be you ought to have it in a regular Middle-
Age house, — Elizabethan or Mary Annean, or whatever they call that sort of architecture.   You could
easily build such a house — something like that incon-
venient edifice put up by the English commissioners at
the Centennial Exhibition ; and if you want to sell this
house " ——

" Which I don't," I replied quickly.   " If I do any
thing, I'll alter this place.   I'm not going to build
another."

As I said, this speech of Tom's disturbed us ; and
after talking about the matter for some days we determined to be consistent, and we had our house altered
so that Tom declared it was a regular Eastlake house
and no mistake.   We had a doleful time while the
alterations were going on ; and when all was done and
we had settled down to quiet again, we missed very
many of the comforts and conveniences to which we
had been accustomed.   But we were getting used to
missing comfort ; and so we sat and looked out of our
little square window-panes, and tried to think the landscape as lovely and the sky as spacious and blue as
when we viewed it through our high and wide French-
plate windows.

But the landscape did not look very well, for it was not the right kind of a landscape. We altered our garden and lawn, and made "pleached alleys" and formal garden-rows and other old-time arrangements.

And so, in time, we had an establishment which was consistent, — it all matched the fire-screen, or rather the frame for a fire-screen.

It might now be supposed that Tom would let us rest a while. But he did nothing of the kind.

"I tell you what it is," said he. "There's just one thing more that you need. You ought to wear clothes to suit the house and furniture. If you'd get an East-lake coat, with a tile set in the back " —— -

This was too much; I interrupted him.

That evening I took our fire-screen and I turned it around. There was a blank expanse on the back of it, and on this I painted, with a brush and some black paint, — with which my wife had been painting storks on some odd-shaped red clay pottery, — the following lines from Dante's "Inferno:"

> "Soltaro finichezza poldo viner
> Glabo icce suzza sil
> Valuchicho mazza churi
> Provenza succi—y gli."

This is intended to mean:

> "Why, oh, why have I taken
> And thrown away my comfort on earth,
> And descended into an old-fashioned hell !"

But as I do not understand Italian it is not likely that any of the words I wrote are correct; but it makes no difference, as so few persons understand the language

and I can always tell them what I meant the inscription
to mean. The " y " and the " gli " are real Italian
and I will not attempt to translate them — but they
look well and give an air of proper construction to the
whole. I might have written the thing in Old English,
but that is harder for me than Italian. The transla-
tion, which is my own, I tried to make, as nearly as
possible, consistent with Dante's poem.

A few days after this I went over to Tom's house.
A brighter, cosier house you never saw. I threw
myself into one of my ex-arm-chairs. I lay back; I
stretched out my legs under a table, — I could never
stretch out my legs under one of my own tables because
they had heavy Eastlake bars under them, and you had
to sit up and keep your legs at an Eastlake angle. I
drew a long sigh of satisfaction. Around me were all
the pretty, tasteful, unsuitable things that Tom had
bought from us — at eighty-seven per cent off. Our
own old spirit of home comfort seemed to be here. I
sprang from my chair.

" Tom," I cried, " what will you take for this house,
this furniture — every thing just as it stands? "

Tom named a sum. I closed the bargain.

We live in Tom's house now, and two happier people
are not easily found. Tom wanted me to sell him my
re-modelled house, but I wouldn't do it. He would
alter things. I rent it to him : and he has to live there,
for he can get no other house in the neighborhood.
He is not the cheerful fellow he used to be, but his wife
comes over to see us very often.

A PIECE OF RED CALICO.

MR. EDITOR: If the following true experience shall prove of any advantage to any of your readers, I shall be glad.

I was going into town the other morning, when my wife handed me a little piece of red calico, and asked me if I would have time, during the day, to buy her two yards and a half of calico like that. I assured her that it would be no trouble at all; and putting the piece of calico in my pocket, I took the train for the city.

At lunch-time I stopped in at a large dry-goods store to attend to my wife's commission. I saw a well-dressed man walking the floor between the counters, where long lines of girls were waiting on much longer lines of customers, and asked him where I could see some red calico.

"This way, sir," and he led me up the store. "Miss Stone," said he to a young lady, "show this gentleman some red calico."

"What shade do you want?" asked Miss Stone.

I showed her the little piece of calico that my wife

had given me. She looked at it and handed it back to me. Then she took down a great roll of red calico and spread it out on the counter.

" Why, that isn't the shade! " said I.

" No, not exactly," said she ; " but it is prettier than your sample."

" That may be," said I ; " but, you see, 1 want to match this piece. There is something already made of this kind of calico, which needs to be made larger, or mended, or something. I want some calico of the same shade."

The girl made no answer, but took down another roll.

" That's the shade," said she.

" Yes," I replied, " but it's striped.

" Stripes are more worn than any thing else in calicoes," said she.

" Yes ; but this isn't to be worn. It's for furniture, I think. At any rate, I want perfectly plain stuff, to match something already in use."

" Well, I don't think you can find it perfectly plain, unless you get Turkey red."

" What is Turkey red? " I asked.

" Turkey red is perfectly plain in calicoes," she answered.

" Well, let me see some."

" We haven't any Turkey red calico left," she said, " but we have some very nice plain calicoes in other colors."

" I don't want any other color. I want stuff to match this."

"It's hard to match cheap calico like that," she said, and so I left her.

I next went into a store a few doors farther up Broadway. When I entered I approached the "floor-walker," and handing him my sample, said:

"Have you any calico like this?"

"Yes, sir," said he. "Third counter to the right."

I went to the third counter to the right, and showed my sample to the salesman in attendance there. He looked at it on both sides. Then he said:

"We haven't any of this."

"That gentleman said you had," said I.

"We had it, but we're out of it now. You'll get that goods at an upholsterer's."

I went across the street to an upholsterer's.

"Have you any stuff like this?" I asked.

"No," said the salesman. "We haven't. Is it for furniture?"

"Yes," I replied.

"Then Turkey red is what you want?"

"Is Turkey red just like this?" I asked.

"No," said he; "but it's much better."

"That makes no difference to me," I replied. "I want something just like this."

"But they don't use that for furniture," he said.

"I should think people could use any thing they wanted for furniture," I remarked, somewhat sharply.

"They can, but they don't," he said quite calmly. "They don't use red like that. They use Turkey red."

I said no more, but left. The next place I visited was a very large dry-goods store. Of the first salesman I saw I inquired if they kept red calico like my sample.

"You'll find that on the second story," said he.

I went up-stairs. There I asked a man:

"Where will I find red calico?"

"In the far room to the left. Right over there." And he pointed to a distant corner.

I walked through the crowds of purchasers and salespeople, and around the counters and tables filled with goods, to the far room to the left. When I got there I asked for red calico.

"The second counter down this side," said the man."

I went there and produced my sample. "Calicoes down-stairs," said the man.

"They told me they were up here," I said.

"Not these plain goods. You'll find 'em down-stairs at the back of the store, over on that side.

I went down-stairs to the back of the store.

"Where will I find red calico like this?" I asked.

"Next counter but one," said the man addressed, walking with me in the direction pointed out.

"Dunn, show red calicoes."

Mr. Dunn took my sample and looked at it.

"We haven't this shade in that quality of goods," he said.

"Well, have you it in any quality of goods?" I asked.

"Yes; we've got it finer." And he took down a piece of calico, and unrolled a yard or two of it on the counter.

" That's not this shade," I said.

" No," said he. " The goods is finer and the color's better."

" I want it to match this," I said.

" I thought you weren't particular about the match," said the salesman. " You said you didn't care for the quality of the goods, and you know you can't match goods without you take into consideration quality and color both. If you want that quality of goods in red, you ought to get Turkey red."

I did not think it necessary to answer this remark, but said :

" Then you've got nothing to match this? "

" No, sir. But perhaps they may have it in the upholstery department, in the sixth story."

So I got in the elevator and went up to the top of the house.

" Have you any red stuff like this? " I said to a young man.

" Red stuff? Upholstery department, — other end of this floor."

I went to the other end of the floor.

" I want some red calico," I said to a man.

" Furniture goods? " he asked.

" Yes," said I.

" Fourth counter to the left."

I went to the fourth counter to the left, and showed my sample to a salesman. He looked at it, and said :

" You'll get this down on the first floor — calico department."

I turned on my heel, descended in the elevator, and

went out on Broadway. I was thoroughly sick of red calico. But I determined to make one more trial. My wife had bought her red calico not long before, and there must be some to be had somewhere. I ought to have asked her where she bought it, but I thought a simple little thing like that could be bought anywhere.

I went into another large dry-goods store. As I entered the door a sudden tremor seized me. I could not bear to take out that piece of red calico. If I had had any other kind of a rag about me — a pen-wiper or any thing of the sort — I think I would have asked them if they could match that.

But I stepped up to a young woman and presented my sample, with the usual question.

" Back room, counter on the left," she said.

I went there.

" Have you any red calico like this?" I asked of the lady behind the counter.

" No, sir," she said, " but we have it in Turkey red."

Turkey red again! I surrendered.

" All right," I said, " give me Turkey red."

" How much, sir? " she asked.

" I don't know — say five yards."

The lady looked at me rather strangely, but measured off five yards of Turkey red calico. Then she rapped on the counter and called out " cash ! " A little girl, with yellow hair in two long plaits, came slowly up. The lady wrote the number of yards, the name of the goods, her own number, the price, the amount of the bank-note I handed her, and some other matters, probably the color of my eyes, and the direction and velocity of the wind, on a slip of paper. She then copied all this in a little book which she kept by her. Then she handed the slip of paper, the money, and the Turkey red to the yellow-haired girl. This young girl copied the slip in a little book she carried, and then she went away with the calico, the paper slip, and the money.

After a very long time, — during which the little girl probably took the goods, the money, and the slip to some central desk, where the note was received, its amount and number entered in a book, change given to the girl, a copy of the slip made and entered, girl's entry examined and approved, goods wrapped up, girl registered, plaits counted and entered on a slip of paper and copied by the girl in her book, girl taken to a hydrant and washed, number of towel entered on a paper slip and copied by the girl in her book, value of my note and amount of change branded somewhere on the child, and said process noted on a slip of paper and copied in her book, — the girl came to me, bringing my change and the package of Turkey red calico.

I had time for but very little work at the office that afternoon, and when I reached home, I handed the package of calico to my wife. She unrolled it and exclaimed :

" Why, this don't match the piece I gave you ! "

" Match it ! " I cried. " Oh, no ! it don't match it. You didn't want that matched. You were mistaken. What you wanted was Turkey red — third counter to the left. I mean, Turkey red is what they use."

My wife looked at me in amazement, and then I detailed to her my troubles.

"Well," said she, "this Turkey red is a great deal prettier than what I had, and you've got so much of it that I needn't use the other at all. I wish I had thought of Turkey red before."

"I wish from my heart you had," said I.

ANDREW SCOGGIN

EVERY MAN HIS OWN LETTER-WRITER.

[Mr. Editor: I find, in looking over the various "Complete Letter-writers," where so many persons of limited opportunities find models for their epistolary correspondence, that there are many contingencies incident to our social and domestic life which have not been provided for in any of these books. I therefore send you a few models of letters suitable to various occasions, which I think may be found useful. I have endeavored, as nearly as possible, to preserve the style and diction in use in the ordinary "Letter-writers."

Yours, etc.,　F. R. S.]

No. 1.

From a little girl living with an unmarried aunt, to her mother, the widow of a Unitarian clergyman, who is engaged as matron of an Institution for Deaf Mutes, in Wyoming Territory.

New Brunswick, N.J., Aug. 12th, 1877.

Revered Parent: As the morning sun rose, this day, upon the sixth anniversary, both of my birth and of my introduction to one who, though separated from me by vast and apparently limitless expanses of territory, is not only my maternal parent but my most trustworthy coadjutor in all points of duty, propriety and social responsibility, I take this opportunity of assuring you of the tender and sympathetic affection I feel for you, and of the earnest solicitude with which I ever regard you. I take pleasure in communicating the intelligence of my admirable physical condition, and hoping that you will continue to preserve the highest degree of health compatible with your age and arduous duties, I am,

Your affectionate and dutiful daughter,

MARIA STANLEY.

No. 2.

From a young gentleman, who having injured the muscles of the back of his neck by striking them while swimming, on a pane of glass, shaken from the window of a fore-and-aft schooner, by a severe collision with a wagon loaded with stone, which had been upset in a creek, in reply to a cousin by marriage who invites him to invest his savings in a patent machine for the disintegration of mutton suet.

BELLEVILLE HOSPITAL, CENTER Co., O.,
Jan. 12, 1877.

MY RESPECTED COUSIN: The incoherency of your request with my condition [*here state the condition*] is so forcibly impressed upon my sentient faculties [*enumerate and define the faculties*] that I cannot refrain from endeavoring to avoid any hesitancy in making an effort to produce the same or a similar impression upon your perceptive capabilities. With kindest regards for the several members of your household [*indicate the members*], I am ever,

Your attached relative,

MARTIN JORDAN.

No. 3.

From a superintendent of an iron-foundery, to a lady who refused his hand in her youth, and who has since married an inspector of customs in one of the southern states, requesting her, in case of her husband's decease, to give him permission to address her, with a view to a matrimonial alliance.

BRIER IRON MILLS, Secauqua, Ill., July 7, '77.

DEAR MADAM: Although I am fully aware of the robust condition of your respected husband's health, and of your tender affection for him and your little ones, I am impelled by a sense of the propriety of providing in time for the casualties and fortuities of the future, to ask of you permission, in case of your (at present unexpected) widowhood, to renew the addresses which were broken off by your marriage to your present estimable consort.

An early answer will oblige,

Yours respectfully,
JOHN PICKETT.

No. 4.

From a cook-maid in the family of a dealer in silverplated casters, to the principal of a boarding-school, enclosing the miniature of her suitor.

1317 EAST 17TH ST., N.Y., July 30, '77.

VENERATED MADAM : The unintermittent interest you have perpetually indicated in the direction of my wellbeing stimulates me to announce my approaching conjugal association with a gentleman fully my peer in all that regards social position or mental aspiration, and, at the same time, to desire of you, in case of the abrupt dissolution of the connection between myself and my present employers, that you will permit me to perform, for a suitable remuneration, the lavatory processes necessary for the habiliments of your pupils.

Your respectful well-wisher,
SUSAN MAGUIRE.

No. 5.

From a father to his son at school, in answer to a letter asking for an increase of pocket-money.

My Dear Joseph : Your letter asking for an augmentation of your pecuniary stipend has been received, together with a communication from your preceptor, relative to your demeanor at the seminary.   Permit me to say, that should I ever again peruse an epistle similar to either of these, you may confidently anticipate, on your return to my domicile, an excoriation of the cuticle which will adhere to your memory for a term of years.

Your affectionate father,
HENRY BAILEY.

No. 6.

From the author of a treatise on molecular subdivision, who has been rejected by the daughter of a cascarilla-bark-refiner, whose uncle has recently been paid sixty-three dollars for repairing a culvert in Indianapolis, to the tailor of a converted Jew on the eastern shore

*of Maryland, who has requested the loan of a hypo-
dermic syringe.*

WEST ORANGE, Jan. 2, 1877.

DEAR SIR: Were it not for unexpected obstacles,
which have most unfortuitously arisen, to a connection which I hoped, at an early date, to announce, but
which, now, may be considered, by the most sanguine
observer, as highly improbable, I might have been able
to obtain a pecuniary loan from a connection of the
parties with whom I had hoped to be connected, which
would have enabled me to redeem, from the hands of
an hypothecater the instrument you desire, but which
now is as unattainable to you as it is to

Yours most truly,

THOMAS FINLEY.

No. 7.

*From an embassador to Tunis, who has become deaf in
his left ear, to the widow of a manufacturer of perforated under-clothing, whose second son has never
been vaccinated.*

TUNIS, AFRICA, Aug. 3, '77.

MOST HONORED MADAM: Permit me, I most earnestly implore of you, from the burning sands of this
only too far distant foreign clime to call to the notice
of your reflective and judicial faculties the fact that
there are actions which may be deferred until too
recent a period.

With the earnest assurance of my most distinguished
regard, I am, most honored and exemplary madam,
your obedient servant to command,

L. GRANVILLE TIBBS.

No. 8.

From a hog-and-cattle reporter on a morning paper,
who has just had his hair cut by a barber whose father
fell off a wire-bridge in the early part of 1867, to a
gardener, who has written to him that a tortoise-shell
cat, belonging to the widow of a stage-manager, has
dug up a bed of calceolarias, the seed of which had
been sent him by the cashier of a monkey-wrench
factory, which had been set on fire by a one-armed
tramp, whose mother had been a sempstress in the
family of a Hicksite Quaker.

NEW YORK, Jan. 2, '77.

DEAR SIR: In an immense metropolis like this,
where scenes of woe and sorrow meet my pitying
eye at every glance, and where the living creatures,
the observation and consideration of which give me
the means of maintenance, are, always, if deemed in a
proper physical condition, destined to an early grave,
I can only afford a few minutes to condole with you
on the loss you so feelingly announce. These minutes
I now have given.

Very truly yours,

HENRY DAWSON.

No. 9.

From the wife of a farmer, who, having sewed rags
enough to make a carpet, is in doubt whether to
sell the rags, and with the money buy a mince-meat
chopper and two cochin-china hens of an old lady,
who, having been afflicted with varicose veins, has
determined to send her nephew, who has been working
for a pump-maker in the neighboring village, but who

*comes home at night to sleep, to a school kept by a
divinity student whose father has been educated by the
clergyman who had married her father and mother,
and to give up her little farm and go to East Dur-
ham, N. Y., to live with a cousin of her mother,
named Amos Murdock, or to have the carpet made
up by a weaver who had bought oats from her husband, for a horse which had been lent to him for his
keep — being a little tender in his fore-feet — by a city
doctor, but who would still owe two or three dollars
after the carpet was woven, and keep it until her
daughter, who was married to a dealer in second-
hand blowing-engines for agitating oil, should come
to make her a visit, and then put it down in her
second-story front chamber, with a small piece of
another rag-carpet, which had been under a bed, and
was not worn at all, in a recess which it would be a
pity to cut a new carpet to fit, to an unmarried sister
who keeps house for an importer of Limoges faïence.*

GREENVILLE, July 20, '77.

DEAR MARIA : Now that my winter labors, so un-
avoidably continued through the vernal season until
now, are happily concluded, I cannot determine, by
any mental process with which I am familiar, what
final disposition of the proceeds of my toil would be
most conducive to my general well-being. If, therefore, you will bend the energies of your intellect upon
the solution of this problem, you will confer a most
highly appreciated favor upon

Your perplexed sister,

AMANDA DANIELS.

Printed in the United States
80475LV00006B/104

9 781417 926817